"WON'T YOU JOIN ME?"

Fargo looked at Carrie, offering her a cup of the Indian mescal.

"I'd rather not. I've already tasted it, thank you."

Fargo smiled and tossed the liquor down. The mescal singed his tonsils, then burned a fiery path all the way down to his stomach. With wide, appreciative eyes, he poured himself another drink. As he lifted the cup to his lips, she reached over and gently took his hand.

"Isn't that supposed to make a man . . . Well, you know."

He saw her meaning at once. She was wrong, of course. A good powerful brew never stopped him. Putting down his drink, Fargo pushed himself erect. Carrie smiled up at him and kissed him hungrily, in a steaming fury of impatience . . .

Exciting Westerns by Jon Sharpe

THE TRAILSMAN 32

APACHE GOLD

by
Jon Sharpe

A SIGNET BOOK

NEW AMERICAN LIBRARY

NAL BOOKS ARE AVAILABLE AT QUANTITY DISCOUNTS
WHEN USED TO PROMOTE PRODUCTS OR SERVICES.
FOR INFORMATION PLEASE WRITE TO PREMIUM MARKETING DIVISION,
NEW AMERICAN LIBRARY, 1633 BROADWAY,
NEW YORK, NEW YORK 10019.

Copyright © 1984 by Jon Sharpe

The first chapter of this book appeared in *Six-Gun Sombreros*,
the thirty-first volume in this series.

SIGNET TRADEMARK REG. U.S. PAT. OFF. AND FOREIGN COUNTRIES
REGISTERED TRADEMARK—MARCA REGISTRADA
HECHO EN CHICAGO, U.S.A.

SIGNET, SIGNET CLASSIC, MENTOR, PLUME, MERIDIAN
AND NAL BOOKS
are published by
New American Library,
1633 Broadway,
New York, New York 10019

First Printing, August, 1984

1   2   3   4   5   6   7   8   9

PRINTED IN THE UNITED STATES OF AMERICA

The Trailsman

Beginnings . . . they bend the tree and they
mark the man. Skye Fargo was born when he
was eighteen. Terror was his midwife,
vengeance his first cry. Killing spawned Skye
Fargo, ruthless, cold-blooded murder. Out of
the acrid smoke of gunpowder still hanging in
the air, he rose, cried out a promise never
forgotten.

The Trailsman, they began to call him all
across the West, searcher, scout, hunter, the man
who could see where others only looked, his
skills for hire but not his soul, the man who lived
each day to the fullest, yet trailed each
tomorrow. Skye Fargo, the Trailsman, the seeker
who could take the wildness of a land and the
wanting of a woman and make them his own.

*Gold City, deep in Arizona Territory,
where Apache gold and miners' blood are mingling . . .*

1

Skye Fargo sat up, suddenly alert.

"What's the matter, honey?" the buxom blonde asked, lifting her head and staring up at him. "There ain't no need for you stop now. You doin' just great."

"Downstairs. That racket in the saloon. A chair breaking, I think."

Then came the sound of heavy, running feet.

Moving with the speed and grace of a mountain cat, Fargo left the bed and hurried to the window. Peering down, he saw men just below him running from the Miner's Haven saloon, others rushing toward it. A shoot-out was coming, maybe. Fargo didn't like that. The floors in this boom-town saloon were as flimsy as the walls and offered almost no protection from flying bullets.

As Fargo pulled away from the window, his lean face crinkled into a devilish grin. Sometimes trouble had a way of clearing his head like a drink of cold, fresh, spring water.

"There's trouble brewing downstairs," he told the blonde. "I'll be right back."

Disappointment clouded her face as she sat up and watched him, her eyes feasting on his nakedness. "Honey," she said, "let them fight. What's that got to do with us?"

"If they start shooting down there, we're liable to catch a stray slug. Or a lamp could overturn and start a fire." He winked at her. "I was planning on spending the night here with you, remember."

A shade over six feet tall, Skye Fargo was big enough to hunt bears with a switch. As he plucked his buckskin pants off the chair and got ready to step into them, a bear-claw scar in the shape of a half-moon became visible on his forearm, while the muscles on his massive shoulders and torso stood out like mole tunnels. His unruly black hair—the color of a raven's wing—hung almost to his shoulders.

Buttoning up his fly, Fargo had a momentary problem with a portion of his anatomy that refused to believe he was not staying in bed with the blonde. Watching him from the bed, the blonde was having trouble with the idea also.

"See how that big feller don't want to go down, honey," she said, pouting. "Why don't you just stay up here with me?"

Grinning, Fargo turned and strode back to her. Sweeping up one ample breast in his big palm, he kissed the nipple. "I won't be goin' far, Rose. I

10

promise you. When I get back, you'll be glad I went. You stay right where you are. Hear?"

The blonde nodded doubtfully and slid down under the sheet, her eyes watching him curiously as he slipped out the door.

From the stairway's first-floor landing, Fargo paused and looked down at the crowded bar. He had guessed right. There was trouble, all right. A chair was overturned and in the center of the room two men were slowly circling each other. Around them, forming a ring of spectators, stood the saloon's patrons, their jaws slack, their eyes filled with a blood lust. Like a wolf pack circling a crippled doe, they were waiting for the kill.

Fargo had just ridden into Gold City only a few days before, but already he knew the two men squaring off. The smaller of the two was Rex Barry, a Wells Fargo shotgun messenger. White-haired and in his fifties, he was shorter by a foot than the other one. In a worn leather holster he carried an ancient Colt. Fargo had shared a couple of drinks with him earlier in the day and liked him.

The other one was Slade Kingston, a gambler recently arrived from a Mississippi steamboat. Fargo had disliked him almost from the first. And he was almost certain Slade had not dealt every card from the top of the deck while playing poker with Fargo that afternoon. But Fargo had had other irons in the fire at the time and had not challenged him.

Fargo saw clearly what must have just happened. Rex Barry had accused the gambler of cheating and now Slade was bullying him into a gunfight, which could have only one outcome. The white-haired shotgun messenger was no gunfighter.

Fargo started down the stairs.

He had almost reached the saloon floor when the two men stopped circling each other and Slade Kingston's sharp, grating voice boomed out in the hushed saloon.

"You heard me, Barry! I expect an apology."

"I slapped you 'cause you deserved it, Slade," Barry said, edging back. "You called me a fool and a poor loser."

Slade's eyebrows went up slightly. "And you implied I hadn't been playing fair."

"If the shoe fits."

"You are scum, sir. I demand satisfaction."

"You won't get any apology from me," Barry replied stoutly.

Slade dropped his hand to the grips of his gleaming, pearl-handled Colt .45. The ring of spectators pushed back quickly.

"You're wearing a gun, Barry," Slade said. "I expect you'd better get ready to use it."

"You can't make me draw, Slade."

Fargo was not armed, and before he could do anything, Slade drew his Colt. It was a fast draw, lightning-fast.

Barry flung both hands up over his head. "No, Slade," the man cried. "I told you. I won't draw."

Slade appeared ready to shoot anyway, the muzzle of his Colt aimed at Barry's midsection. Barry began to sweat, but he did not crawl.

Abruptly, Slade lowered his Colt, then strode

over to Barry and slammed the old man brutally on the side of the head. Barry's hat went flying as he toppled like a tree, his head knocking a cuspidor to one side as it crunched onto the floor. Blood oozed thickly from a deep gash over the old man's temple.

Slade stepped back, then kicked Barry viciously in the side. Barry groaned slightly and raised a forearm in a feeble attempt to ward off the next blow.

It never came.

Fargo had reached Slade Kingston by that time. He caught Slade's right arm and spun him around. Slade was a dandy, his full head of dark hair well-groomed, his mustache closely trimmed. He was wearing a black frock coat and tan trousers that followed closely the line of his calves. His boots were highly polished.

"Back off, Slade," Fargo told him.

Kingston pulled himself angrily out of Fargo's grasp. "This isn't your affair," he said, his dark eyes snapping angrily.

"I just dealt myself in."

"You're a fool, then."

"You calling me a fool, are you? Now *I* want satisfaction."

Kingston glanced contemptuously down at Fargo's waist. "You aren't armed."

"Sure, I am," Fargo said, holding up his two fists.

"I am a gentleman, sir. It is not my practice to brawl with half-naked louts."

"I see. You just cheat at cards and beat up old men. Is that it?"

Kingston's cruelly handsome face went pale. Fargo smiled, enjoying Slade's discomfiture. "Later, Fargo," the gambler managed, turning his back on Fargo and striding over to the bar. "Later. You'll get your turn. I promise you."

"Sure, Slade. But I'm warning you. The next time you play cards with me, you'd better keep both hands on the table—and your sleeves empty."

At this second, deliberate insult, the gambler's shoulders stiffened. He placed both hands palms down on the top of the bar to steady himself, then glanced in the mirror behind the bar as he addressed Fargo. "I know what your intentions are," he said, "but I will not be provoked."

Fargo walked up behind Slade, grabbed him by the shoulder, and spun him around. Then he slapped him—hard. Tears of rage flooded Slade's eyes. This time Slade went for his gun, but Fargo caught his right wrist and twisted. Gasping, Slade went down on one knee. Fargo lifted the gun from Slade's holster and flung it across the room. Then he hauled Slade to his feet, turned him roughly, and with a powerful kick sent him windmilling out through the batwing doors. From outside the saloon came the sharp crack of a hitch rail snapping under Slade's weight, followed by the whinnying of startled horses rearing and clattering away from the front of the saloon.

Fargo turned around then and walked over to the still-unconscious Rex Barry. He picked Barry up and carried him in his arms over to a faro table. The entire right side of the shotgun messenger's face

14

was encased in a dark shell of coagulating blood. Fargo thought there was a good chance the old man's skull had been fractured.

Putting Barry down gently on the faro table, Fargo turned to those men crowding around. "Get a doctor!"

Someone in the rear of the crowd turned and bolted from the saloon. By this time, the saloon was filled with excited patrons, who now crowded around Fargo, their faces beaming, their hands reaching out to shake his hand or slap him on the back.

Pulling back from the crowd, Fargo looked around into their faces and said quietly, "Not a single one of you made a move to help this man."

"It wasn't our fight."

"Yeah!" said another. "He accused Kingston of cheating."

"You know he does," Fargo reminded them. "Even so, you all just stood around gaping."

"That ain't fair, mister."

"How fair was it when Slade clubbed Barry to the ground?"

To that there was only a sullen, cowed silence.

Those standing closest to Fargo glanced uneasily at one another and took a step back. The men behind them moved back also, avoiding Fargo's quietly accusing eyes as they did so. A few moistened their lips to say something, then thought better of it. The crowd broke up then as some men hurried from the saloon, while others hunched up to the bar like whipped children.

Abruptly, the fellow who had gone for the doctor returned with a tall, spare, white-haired man with alert eyes peering out from behind steel-rimmed spectacles. The doctor hurried over to the faro table and immediately bent to examine Barry. After a thorough, meticulous examination, he glanced up at Fargo, a frown on his face.

"Is he going to be all right?" Fargo asked the doctor.

"He has a mild concussion, but it could get worse, much worse, if he doesn't keep himself quiet. I'll need help to move him to his room."

Fargo's eyes caught those of two husky-looking men sitting at a nearby table. One glance was all that was needed. The two patrons got hastily to their feet and, under the doctor's direction, helped carry the still-unconscious shotgun messenger from the saloon.

That accomplished, Fargo purchased a bottle of bourbon and hurried back up the stairs to Rose. When he reentered her room a moment later and locked the door behind him, she glanced over at him somewhat apprehensively. He smiled as he put the bottle on the floor near the bed and swiftly peeled off his britches and climbed into bed beside her. Sighing in relief, she spread herself happily to receive him. Ready in seconds, he entered her lush warmth easily, plunging deep. She gasped in delight as she took all of him.

"Go deeper!" she gasped.

"How's that?"

"Deeper!"

16

He obliged, the anger he felt fading now.

"Mmmm!" she murmured. "Oh, yes, yes!"

A moment later Rose screamed and flung her arms around his neck. But he didn't let up. He just kept driving.

2

The next morning Rose and Fargo were having breakfast in a restaurant across the street from the saloon when a tall fellow dressed in a well-tailored dark suit strode into the place. He was obviously looking for someone, and when he spotted Fargo, he headed immediately for his table. Fargo knew him as Tim Bridger, the Wells Fargo agent in Gold City.

"Sit down," said Fargo. "Join us."

"I already had breakfast, Fargo," Bridger said. His voice was unpleasantly officious. And he refused even to acknowledge Rose's presence at the table. "But maybe I'll join you in coffee."

"Suit yourself."

Bridger sat down at the table, still careful to avoid Rose's gaze. He was wearing a black stetson. This, combined with his black suit and the somber, almost melancholy cast to his features, made for a somewhat funereal appearance and tended to dampen Fargo's enthusiasm for the bright morning. The Wells Fargo agent did not look healthy. Despite his full, sensual lips, his hollow cheeks and brooding eyes set deep in their sockets gave him an almost cadaverous appearance.

After the waitress brought his coffee, Bridger cleared his throat. "Rex is still hurt pretty bad, Fargo," he said. "But Dr. McIntosh says he'll be all right if he gives himself a rest."

Fargo nodded. He had figured as much.

"I came over to ask if you'd do me—that is, Wells Fargo—a favor," Bridger said.

Fargo glanced up from his steak, a gleam in his lake-blue eyes. "I already did my good deed for the week."

"I know that, Fargo, and we all appreciate your standing up to Slade Kingston like that. Nevertheless, we are still left with a problem."

"I'm listenin'."

"We need a man to ride shotgun."

"Just on this run?"

"That's right," Bridger said.

The Trailsman frowned and put down his knife and fork. He did not wish to appear anxious, but it had immediately occurred to him that this might fit quite nicely into his plans. He had come to Arizona because he knew this particular stage route was being looted systematically by the Bart Mullin gang, one member of which seemed to fit the description of one of those men Fargo was searching for—a member of a gang of highwaymen who many years before had killed his entire family.

"What's the pay?" Fargo asked cautiously.

"On this trip?"

Fargo nodded.

"Five dollars a day."

"That's pretty steep, ain't it? You expecting a war to break out?"

"There have been several holdups in the past month. Wells Fargo is determined to protect its coaches, and you seem to be a man capable of giving it that protection."

"I'll need a Greener."

"You can use Rex's. He sure as hell won't be needing it for a while."

"When's the stage pulling out?"

"In an hour."

"That doesn't give me much time."

Bridger shrugged.

Rose spoke up then. "Word around town is there's a big gold shipment going out today."

Bridger looked at Rose for the first time. It was obvious he did not approve of her—or her profession, at least not while he was cold sober. "Fool talk," he snapped at her. "The same talk that's been going around for weeks."

"Then there's nothing of any value being shipped today?" Fargo asked.

"I didn't say that. There's always valuables, on every run. That's why we have a strongbox."

Fargo nodded, studying Bridger's face—and eyes—intently. He didn't like the evasiveness he sensed in them.

"Well?" Bridger asked. "Will you take the job?"

"Sure. At five dollars a day, how can I go wrong?"

Bridger finished his coffee and stood up. "Fine. I'll tell Bill Gifford. He'll be the jehu on this run."

Fargo nodded. As Bridger turned and started from the restaurant, Fargo got to his feet. "Just a minute, Bridger," he said softly.

Bridger pulled up and swung around, a frown on his face. "What do you want, Fargo?" he asked.

Fargo smiled. "You have lousy manners, Bridger. You forgot to greet my breakfast guest when you sat down. Then you forgot to bid her good day when you left. I'm sure it was just an oversight."

Bridger swallowed angrily and seemed about to make some kind of sarcastic remark, but the cold light in Fargo's eyes restrained him. He doffed his hat, bowed politely to Rose, and said, "Good day, ma'am."

Rose smiled and inclined her head slightly.

Swinging back around angrily, Bridger strode from the restaurant.

Rose shuddered and smiled gratefully at Fargo. "You shouldn't have done that," she said. "But thank you."

"A Wells Fargo agent should have better manners, Rose. He needs to be taken to school on that account, seems to me,"

Rose nodded. "He's a strange one, all right. From what I hear, he used to be a preacher. Some who heard him said he was quite a fire-breather."

Fargo nodded. He wasn't surprised. He had recognized in the express agent's grim, disapproving manner the hostility of a fanatic—a type Fargo never found easy to trust.

"He gives me the creeps sometimes," Rose went on. "I can feel his eyes on me whenever I pass the express office."

"Don't worry about him."

"Oh, I won't, Fargo. I'm leaving Gold City in a couple of days. I have a friend in Denver. She's opening a fine house there. I'll be glad to shake this grubby place."

"I'll miss you."

"It is nice of you to say that," she replied, smiling warmly.

"I mean it."

"Of course. Now finish your breakfast. You've got a stage to catch."

Yes, Fargo thought, returning to his steak. Rose was right. He had come to Gold City in search of a man, and it looked as if the Wells Fargo agent had just given him the opportunity he needed to find the bastard.

Fargo took his Ovaro out of the livery stable and rode him over to the Wells Fargo horse barn. He told the hostler, Sim Tompkins, that if he didn't take good care of the pinto until he got back, Fargo would force-feed him a bucket full of oats—without water. Fargo grinned when he said this, but Tompkins understood perfectly. Fargo was most anxious to see to it that his pinto was well taken care of while he was on this run.

"He's a damn pretty Ovaro," Tompkins commented, patting the horse's neck affectionately.

"Nicest piece of horseflesh I've seen in a long time. Be a pleasure to groom him, Mr. Fargo. He'll be a mite fat and sassy by the time you get back, though. Want me to breeze him out once in a while?"

"Yes, I'd appreciate that," said Fargo. "Just go easy on him. You won't need rowels."

"I can see that."

Fargo left Tompkins and carried his gear over to the waiting stagecoach. A powerful six-horse team had already been backed into the traces and two stable boys were now busy harnessing up the team. Fargo climbed up into the box and stowed his personal gear on the storage rack on top of the coach. Then he clambered down to get the Greener waiting for him in the express office. As he mounted the steps to the office, he encountered the driver just coming out.

"What's going out this morning?" Fargo asked him.

"A whiskey drummer, a mail sack, and a strongbox."

"What's in the strongbox?"

Bill Gifford sent a black dart of tobacco juice out of the corner of his mouth. "Valuables."

"That's not much help, Bill."

"There ain't no gold in it, if that's what you're thinkin'."

With a shrug, Fargo moved past the driver into the office and took down Barry's Greener from the rack. He broke the shotgun to check it out, then looked up at Bridger to ask for shells. The agent was way ahead of him. Without a word, he handed Fargo a small box of shells.

"Thanks, Bridger," Fargo said.

The Wells Fargo agent lifted his face to peer at Fargo, his dark, brooding eyes gleaming with disapproval. Fargo guessed he was still seething inwardly from that scene earlier in the restaurant when he had been forced to bid Rose a polite goodbye.

"Just do your job, Mr. Fargo," he said. "That's all I want from you."

"Fair enough," Fargo said. He turned then and walked back outside to take another look at the stage. The Concord coach's body was painted a bright red, set off by gold trim on all the panels and the door. The leather of the front and rear boots was black and gleaming, the wheels' yellow spokes and rims shining from a recent waxing. The brake shoes looked hardly worn, in fact.

Skip Turpin, the Wells Fargo clerk whom Fargo had met earlier that morning, stepped up onto the porch and paused beside Fargo, admiring with him the bright new stagecoach. Skip was a lanky towhead with a quick, sunny smile.

"She's sure a beauty, ain't she?" Skip said, his hazel eyes gleaming.

"True enough, Skip."

"We spent all night getting her ready."

"It looks it."

As they watched, Bill Gifford left the barn and climbed up into the driver's box.

"Well, good luck, Mr. Fargo," Skip said, smiling.

"I sure admire the way you stood up for Rex yesterday."

"Why, thank you, Skip."

Then, with a nod, Fargo left the clerk, crossed the yard to the stage, and clambered up beside Bill Gifford. "So we're breaking in a brand-new coach, are we?" Fargo commented.

"Yep," Gifford said proudly. "This is her first run. So let's make sure nothin' bad happens to her."

Fargo nodded and looked down once more at the Greener. The shotgun was well-oiled and appeared to be in excellent shape. It did not look as if Rex Barry had ever fired it in anger. This did not lull Fargo, however. Like Rose, he had heard the talk in town about a gold shipment. The way the story went, fear that Bart Mullin's gang would rob the assay office had prompted the Wells Fargo headquarters in San Francisco to direct Bridger to ship out whatever gold ingots they were storing by the earliest possible stage.

Bill Gifford spat a long rope of tobacco juice out of his mouth. He looked fidgety and impatient.

"What are we waiting for?" Fargo asked.

"The sheriff. He's personally escorting a friend of his to the stage."

At that moment Sheriff Charlie Sands appeared, hauling a whiskey drummer down the boardwalk toward the express office. The drummer was walking unsteadily and the sheriff was doing what he could to keep the man upright. The drummer, his white shirt stained and his collar hanging by one button, lost his derby hat twice as the sheriff helped him along. Reaching the coach, the sheriff

25

boosted the inebriated salesman through the door, then looked up at Gifford and Fargo.

The sheriff was a blockily built man with broad, beetling brows and features that seemed squeezed together. At the moment his small dark eyes gleamed with surprising malevolence.

"You two take good care of my friend here," he warned them. "I don't want nothing to happen to him."

"Why don't you ride along," suggested Fargo, "seein' you're that concerned?"

"Do I know you?"

"Name's Fargo, Skye Fargo."

"You're the one faced down Slade Kingston yesterday."

"That's right," said Gifford, "while you was out carousin' with this here whiskey drummer."

"Now, just a minute there."

Ignoring the sheriff's angry response, Gifford fitted the ribbons into his thick, gnarled fingers. "Stand back, Sheriff," he cried. "We got a run to make."

Gifford took his foot off the brake and cursed with full-throated eloquence at his team. Then he sent his whip cracking over the six gleaming backs. The sheriff stepped hastily out of the way as the six powerful horses broke into a trot. Rocking on its leather thoroughbraces, the stage rolled out of town toward a brightening morning sky. It was going to be another hot one, Fargo realized.

Three hours later, the sun was a blazing ingot burning a hole in the back of Fargo's neck. Both he and Gifford were covered from head to foot with alkali dust, their eyes peering through slitted lids at a cruel, brass-yellow world of sun-blasted rock and desert. There had been no peep out of their only passenger since leaving Gold City, and neither one of them had bothered to check on the fellow. Fargo imagined that he was probably stretched out on one of the benches, oblivious to the world he was passing through as he slept off his drunk.

Fargo himself was thinking back on Gold City. He had found it to be a typical boom town, feeding lasciviously and riotously on the gold being panned from the streams nearby. But unlike so many other mining towns, Gold City was filled with a seething resentment that permeated every conversation and hung over the town like a curse.

More than one prospector had returned from the rocky wilderness through which this stagecoach now plunged with tales of streambeds gleaming with gold dust. Yet, with a thoroughness and brutality typical of their kind, the Apaches had so far managed to keep the prospectors from advancing any farther into these mountains.

The result was a town swarming with angry, gold-hungry men who talked and schemed of only one thing: how to drive the damned Apaches from their stronghold. But in the absence of government troops to back their play, none of their harebrained schemes could come to much more than whiskey-fueled bluster. And so the gold-seekers, stymied, were forced to whittle on the boardwalks or swill booze in the saloons, their souls on fire with a desire to get their hands on the gold they imagined was waiting for them just beyond their reach.

Gifford cleared his throat. Fargo looked at him.

"Just thought you ought to know somethin'," the jehu said.

"Go ahead," Fargo shouted above the rattle of the coach.

"Before we left Gold City I got word that Shriber's station was hit by Apaches."

"When?"

"Late yesterday."

"How bad was it?"

"From what I heard, all that's left is a chimney and some well-done corpses that used to work for Wells Fargo. Naratena's band, more'n likely."

"Naratena? Who's he?"

"Apache war chief. He's been doing his best to keep the prospectors out of these mountains. And so far he's been real successful."

"What's he got against stagecoaches?"

"That's what I can't rightly understand. Up until now he's never touched a single Wells Fargo coach or way station—as long as the stage kept to the road and didn't bring in prospectors."

Fargo shrugged. He knew the Apache to be a savage, unforgiving tribe. They made fine distinctions, but no one could tell when they might change their mind.

Abruptly, the stage slammed down into a twisting grade that led between two towering rock pillars. After they rocked on through them, almost at once the horses began a straining upward climb that had Bill Gifford flicking the ribbons constantly.

28

As the stage climbed higher and higher into this rugged upland, Fargo found growing within him a grudging admiration for the wild beauty of this spectacular land of twisting canyons and walls of sheer, polished rock. Fargo saw towering monuments of rock looming out of the landscape on both sides of the trail, some of them resembling prodigious, hunched creatures. Peering at them, Fargo was reminded of lost souls—frozen forever into attitudes of eternal torment.

"Keep your eyes peeled," Bill grumbled, breaking into Fargo's thoughts. "We're comin' into Apache country now."

They came to a sudden downgrade, and Gifford slammed his booted foot onto the brake, keeping it there. At the bottom of the grade, he saw that a sudden downpour had gouged a deep cut across the stage road's twin ruts. He shifted the Greener in his lap as the stage rocked on toward it.

Bill hunched forward almost eagerly as he tightened his grips on the reins. "Steady there!" he cried to his horses. "Keep a-goin', damn you."

The six horses plunged down the near side of the wash. The stage rocked forward dangerously as it plunged crazily down over the cut's rim. With a roar the wheels slammed into the wash's gravel bed. Pebbles and good-sized stones went flying. The coach skittered to one side, and for a moment Fargo was certain it was going to tip over onto its side. But the horses did not falter as Bill shouted to the leaders and urged them on with a scalding mixture of endearments and blasphemies.

Up the far side of the wash the horses lunged,

their powerful muscles bunching, their hooves sending soft clods of dirt flying. They gained the rim, and a second later, rocking dangerously, the stage was pulled out of the wash and lunged, forward, swaying treacherously.

As Bill hauled back on the reins and settled the horses into a more leisurely pace, he turned to Fargo with a pleased grin, his right cheek bulging with his chaw. Then he spat out a long black stream of tobacco juice.

"This here's a great team," he shouted above the roar of the coach. "I picked out each horse myself."

Fargo started to reply, but Bill's right cheekbone vanished. With it went Bill's eye and a portion of his jaw. As the report from the rifle that killed Bill echoed above the rattle of the stage, Bill dropped the reins and tumbled back off the box.

Fargo did not hear the second rifle shot. But he saw a portion of the seat beside him disintegrate as the slug slammed into it. By this time the horses were bolting, the reins having fallen down among the traces. The stage picked up speed precipitously and began to rock wildly along. Another slug whined off the iron railing of the baggage rack. The horses were now galloping full out.

As Fargo tried to climb down onto the traces to grab the reins, the stage's right wheel struck a boulder. The entire coach lifted. Fargo tried to reach back and grab the box, but he missed and went peeling back off the plunging stagecoach. He struck the hard-packed ground a jolting blow, landing on his shoulders. Then his head slammed back.

Lights exploded deep within his skull, and that was all he remembered.

Naratena, the Apache chieftain, had seen it all.

Cradling a gleaming rifle in his arm, he stood erect on the ledge high overhead, watching impassively as first the stage driver, then the shotgun messenger toppled from the stage.

The squat, powerfully built chief was dressed in a buckskin shirt and breechclout. A clean white headband kept his thick, lustrous black hair in place, and on his feet he wore the traditional Apache moccasins, the *n-deh b'keh*, a thigh-length, thick-soled footgear that enabled the Apache warrior to cover seventy miles a day on foot over this cruel and unrelenting ground.

Naratena's face was typical of the Apache—broad and rather flat—except for his dark-blue eyes and sharply prominent nose, legacies of a fierce Spanish grandmother whose voice had always carried weight in tribal council.

Behind Naratena, on a ledge about six feet lower, a line of silent warriors waited. All but two of them carried bright new rifles. The remaining two, the youngest, carried the traditional weapons of the Apache: a rawhide sling, elmwood bow, and deerskin case, and the nine-foot-long war lances tipped with steel blades. The elmwood bows had a lethal range of one hundred yards and their slings were capable of hurling stones at least fifty yards farther. All eighteen of the warriors watched their chief with eager, impatient eyes, like hounds straining on their leashes.

Naratena went down suddenly on one knee and, using his rifle for support, leaned far out over the ledge to see more clearly who had been firing at the stagecoach. What he saw caused him to grunt softly. Then, below him on the stage trail, the stagecoach struck a boulder, careened wildly, and slammed over onto its side, disintegrating as it struck the ground. The horses, terrified, continued on, dragging their traces after them.

Naratena got back up onto his feet, turned to his braves, and waved them off the ledge. Then he followed after them swiftly, silently, his Apache moccasins leaving no trace on the hot stone.

3

Fargo regained consciousness with the impatient cries of men ringing in his ears.

He had landed on his back, the rear of his skull coming down hard on the baked ground. Turning his violently throbbing head, he squinted into the sunlight and saw the wrecked stage about fifty yards farther down the road. One wheel had shattered on a huge boulder, causing the coach to veer sharply and slam into a rock wall. Four men—Bart Mullin's gang, Fargo surmised—were swarming over the wreckage.

He peered closely at each outlaw, his blood pounding in his temple. But after searching each face, he felt again that familiar, numbing despair. The killer who had murdered his family was not a member of this gang. They were all too young.

A few feet from the stage, the whiskey drummer was lying facedown in a dark pool of his own blood. From the way he was sprawled it looked as if he had been shot from behind while running from the wrecked stage. His face was turned in Fargo's direction. In the hard, brilliant light from the sun, Fargo saw clearly the gaping hole in his cheek where the bullet had exited.

The crazed horses were now well out of sight. They must have broken free of their traces, or taken them with them when they left the shattered stage behind. Moving his head slightly, Fargo saw, some distance behind him, the body of Bill Gifford. The stage driver's form seemed to have shrunken under the pitiless gaze of the sun. Fargo glanced skyward. Already the vultures were beginning to circle.

Glancing back at the men clambering into the stage, Fargo wondered if they would notice him if he slipped away into the rocks bordering the stage road. Watching the outlaws carefully, he began to inch toward the rocks, pausing every now and then to rest and make sure his movements had not been noticed.

At last, when he judged himself to be close enough, he scrambled to his feet and dashed into the rocks. The sudden exertion caused his head to rock violently. Bright, painful flashes exploded before his eyes, temporarily blinding him. He hung on until his rocking head calmed down, then peered around a boulder. His flight had gone undetected. The four men were inside the wrecked coach now, and from it came the sound of splintering boards. Occasionally, a piece of floorboard would come flying out.

The sounds from within the wrecked coach ceased. Fargo saw one of the men leap down from the stage and race up a narrow trail. He returned a moment later, leading four pack mules. As soon as the mules reached the stage, the men formed a human chain and began passing gold ingots down from the coach, while one of their number packed the gold into the large, padded leather aparejos the mules were carrying.

The explanation for all this was obvious.

Under the guise of getting the new stagecoach ready for its maiden run, the gold had been hidden under the new coach's floorboards the night before. It had been an elaborate ploy to fool Bart Mullin's highwaymen. Unfortunately, it had not succeeded.

In a moment, Fargo realized, one of the outlaws would glance over and notice that he was no longer lying in the road. Careful not to move his head too swiftly, Fargo looked behind him for a way to the top of the bluff looming over him. His eyes searched the rocky slope until he saw what appeared to be a narrow game trail leading to the top of the bluff.

Using the boulders for cover, he made his way to the foot of the narrow trail and started up the steep slope. The loose talus made the footing treacherous, and at the same time the exertion caused his head to pound unmercifully. He soon found he had to be on guard against overextending himself, for whenever he did, fireworks went off in his skull. More than once he was afraid he was going to black out. He was beginning to realize that coming down on his head like that had given him the grand-daddy of all hangovers. Twice Fargo found himself forced to flatten his body against the face of a rock wall and inch his way along until the trail widened.

Meanwhile, the outlaws continued to loot the stage and load up the mules, the sounds of their jubilant progress coming up to Fargo clearly as he inched along hundreds of feet above them.

He reached the top of the bluff with his mouth as dry as the underside of a rattler, his head pounding mercilessly. Slumping down in a small patch of shade, he closed his eyes for a moment to get his bearings, resting his head back very carefully against the cool, shaded face of a boulder.

It was not long before the sound of horses' hooves clattering over stone far below aroused him. He pushed himself away from the boulder and peered down at the canyon floor. The outlaws had finished looting the stage and were moving off. Two mounted outlaws were on point leading the string of mules, while the remaining two rode drag. As Fargo watched, the small caravan left the road and headed into a narrow canyon that appeared to cut deep into the heart of the badlands.

Fargo pushed himself wearily to his feet, checked his Colt, and started to trot along the top of the bluff after them. His hope was that the heavily laden mules would slow them enough, especially in this hellish heat, to enable Fargo to stay with them until nightfall. Then he could move in on them.

If he could keep this throbbing head of his from

spinning right off his shoulders and leaving him behind . . .

"I'm tellin' you, Bart," Clete Andrews said, turning in his saddle and looking back at the canyon walls closing behind them. "That shotgun messenger was gone when I looked back. Bill Gifford and the Pinkerton were still lying on the road, but there was no sign of the shotgun."

"All right," Bart said. "So he was gone. Now forget it."

"Supposin' he comes after us?"

"Shit, you saw me cut him down. I got him clean. He's out here now without a mount or water to keep him going. And we got his Greener. If he ain't dead now, he'll soon wish he were."

The two outlaws were riding on a low ridge above the mules. Tom Wells and Lonny were leading the mules in the draw behind them. Both men had lifted their bandannas up over their noses to keep out the dust, and the brims of their hats were pulled down to shade their faces and necks from the searing sun.

"Supposin' he trails us to Diablo Canyon and sees where we stash the gold?" Clete persisted.

In exasperation, Bart yanked down his bandanna and pulled his horse to a halt. Clete reined in also, and did the same. He could not help noticing how little like an outlaw chieftain Bart looked. He had a long horse face, teeth that crowded out of his mouth, a receding chin, and watery eyes. Yet Clete, for one, would sure as hell never cross him. He could be as terrible in anger as a rabid dog.

"Then go back," Bart snarled wearily. "Find the son of a bitch and kill him. Otherwise, shut up."

Clete did not like to get Bart riled. But he couldn't shake this feeling he had, this prickling at the back of his neck. It had stuck with him since he left the stage, and it had been getting worse every minute. He was a worrier. He admitted it. The three of them were always ribbing him about it. But hell, he couldn't change now. Besides, a couple of times he was sure he had caught something, the glint of sunlight on a gun barrel—or on the point of an Apache lance. He couldn't be sure which, but he *had* seen something, dammit!

"Well, Clete," Bart demanded, breaking into his thoughts, "what's it to be? You goin' back for that shotgun or not?"

"Let me think on it a minute, Bart," Clete replied. Moistening his cracked lips, he glanced back again, searching the canyon's rim. The shotgun could be up there, he reasoned, tracking them now, this very minute. Even without a horse, he'd be able to follow them. At the pace these mules were taking, he'd have no trouble at all keeping up.

With a sigh, Clete swung back in his saddle and looked at Bart. "All right, I think maybe I'll ride back a ways and have a look-see."

Bart narrowed his eyes and looked at Clete for a minute, his cold eyes calculating. Clete knew that Bart suspected him. But that didn't faze Clete. Bart Mullin was the most suspicious man he'd ever known. He trusted nobody—which was probably why he had lasted so long at this trade.

Abruptly, Bart shrugged. "Go ahead, Clete. No one's stoppin' you."

"Where'll you be campin' tonight?"

"Diablo Canyon."

"You figure you'll make it that far by sundown?"

"You let me worry about that."

"Then I'll meet you there."

"If you don't, we'll move on out without you."

"I said I'll catch up. I ain't goin' far. I just want a look-see." Clete turned his mount and lifted his bandanna over his nose again. As he rode away from Bart, he felt Bart's eyes on his back, but he did his best to ignore it.

Glancing down off the ridge at Tom and Lonny escorting the mules on the trail below, he waved. Though they must have wondered where in hell he was going, they did not bother to wave back.

After a quarter of a mile, Clete followed a bend in the trail and found himself suddenly alone, the canyon's towering, intimidating walls lifting into the shimmering sky. He was no longer so certain this was such a good idea. As he rode, his eyes searched both rims intently. He was still bothered by that sense that someone was up there on the rim peering down at him, watching his every move—and the feeling was getting even more pronounced, not less.

Fargo had long since descended to the canyon floor and had done his best to keep the Mullin gang in sight. But slowly, relentlessly, they had pulled away from him. Fargo was no longer confident he could keep up. Boots were for riding, not walking. Every step he took now was a form of punishment.

And his headache was getting worse, not better.

Suddenly Fargo pulled up and cocked his bared head. The clink of iron on stone came again, from the trail just ahead. A rider was coming.

Fargo glanced to his left. A sheer rock face met his gaze. He looked to his right. On that side the slope was not nearly so steep, and it was pock-marked with rocks and boulders of all sizes, the debris remaining from a fault that had split the can-yon wall a hundred feet up. Fargo scrambled across the canyon floor and up past the boulders. He found a game trail and kept going until he was half-way up the slope. Then he hid behind a clump of scrub juniper and peered down at the canyon floor. The rider was still not in sight.

Though Fargo could not be sure this was a mem-ber of the Mullin gang, he could not afford to take any chances. As the sound of the horse's hooves on the stony ground echoed sharply in the canyon below him, he crouched lower.

The rider appeared. Peering at him closely through eyes that seemed unwilling to focus clearly, Fargo was pretty certain it was one of the outlaws. As the man rode, he shaded his eyes and peered up at the canyon rims on both sides. He wore a fringed deerskin shirt he let hang outside his Levi's. His hair hung down almost past his shoulders from under a black, low-crowned plains-man's hat.

When Fargo saw the hat—and the powerful bay the outlaw was riding—he came to a sudden decision. The combination of the hot sun and his cracked skull were killing him, as were his feet. If he were going to survive, he must have that outlaw's hat along with his mount.

Swiftly, Fargo made his way back down the slope, angling sharply to keep parallel to the rider as he continued on past him down the canyon. When he was within thirty yards or so of him, Fargo pulled out his Colt and came to a halt behind a boulder large enough to give him cover. Unfortunately, his sudden stop caused loose gravel and some talus to start trickling down the slope. In a moment a small avalanche had begun.

At once the rider turned his head, then he reached hastily into his scabbard for his rifle. Fargo stood up then boldly, brought up his Colt, and fired at the outlaw. But he had not counted on his pounding head and what this had been doing to his hand and eye coordination since he regained consciousness. His shot went wild, the round plowing a furrow in the slope less than ten feet away. A quick second shot was even less efficient. Fargo was simply unable to coordinate his right hand with what he saw before him. Each time, just before he squeezed the trigger, his hand wavered wildly.

By this time the outlaw had snapped his rifle to his shoulder. A moment before the rifle barked, Fargo ducked back behind the boulder. A portion of the rock face behind Fargo disintegrated, sending a small explosion of tiny rock shards into the back of his neck. Peering around from behind the boulder, Fargo tried a third shot.

He never saw where the bullet went. The outlaw's rifle cracked again, the round catching Fargo's gun barrel and knocking the weapon completely out of his hand. Withdrawing his stinging hand, he looked down at his numb fingers and was grateful that all five were still intact. He could barely close his fist, however.

And now he had no weapon.

Fargo darted out from behind the boulder and raced back up the slope. The outlaw sent a slug into the ground at his feet, but Fargo kept going, scrambling swiftly higher, despite the near-maddening pain in his skull. Soon he was high enough and the cover of brush and ridges solid enough to prevent the outlaw from getting a clear shot at him. Glancing back, Fargo saw the man dismount and start up the slope after him, six-gun in hand.

By that time Fargo was too exhausted to go much farther. And he could barely see, so frequent were the alternating explosions of light and darkness just behind his eyes caused by his sudden exertion. It felt as if a crew of Chinese coolies were blasting a tunnel through his head.

Slumping wearily to the ground, he leaned his back against the side of a boulder that towered at least thirty feet into the air. It was balanced precariously on a small nipple of cap rock protruding from the side of the slope. Through pain-slitted eyes Fargo saw that the ceaseless, wind-driven sand had sculpted away most of the rock's base. The boulder was sitting in a small saucer of rock no bigger around than a girl's waist.

This gave Fargo an idea.

He struggled to his feet and, despite the pain, focused his eyes and searched the slope below. Soon enough, he made out the figure of the outlaw clawing his way doggedly up the slope toward him. Ducking back behind the boulder, Fargo placed his shoulder against it. He felt the boulder rock slightly, but the exertion caused such an uproar in his head that he was forced to sag to the ground and wait for it to decrease some.

When it had done so, he looked around for a lever and saw a dead limb from an overhanging bristlecone pine resting in a crevice. He pulled the branch out of the crack and found it was thick enough and heavy enough to make a perfect lever. Again he peered down the slope. The outlaw was still coming, and by this time he was directly beneath the boulder.

Fitting the branch in under the boulder, Fargo heaved. The boulder rocked some, but not enough. Not nearly enough. Fargo glanced down the slope again. The outlaw was much closer. In desperation, Fargo closed his eyes and put his right shoulder under the branch and heaved again. The boulder rocked forward slightly, then returned to its original perch. Fargo heaved up on the branch a third time. The boulder seemed to lean farther this time.

Fargo caught on. He had to impart a continuous rocking motion to the boulder. Timing his thrusts carefully, Fargo heaved upward again and again until he had established a kind of rhythm.

But it soon became obvious he was not going to

be able to defeat the boulder's massive inertia with only the leverage he could impart with his branch. Dropping it, he leaned his shoulder back against the boulder's massive side, waited until it began its ponderous, forward motion; then, with all the strength left in his powerful body, he thrust backward. The blood thudded wildly in his temples and he blacked out momentarily. But he kept heaving, his cheek now tucked against the warm, unyielding surface of the boulder. He felt the boulder tremble as it teetered on the lip of the tiny saucer. For an instant, it hesitated. Then it lifted forward, crunched to the ground, and began rolling down the slope.

Panting wildly, sweat pouring off him, Fargo collapsed. The pounding in his head had become like the roaring of an inner avalanche. Ignoring it, he watched through slitted eyelids as the outlaw—less than fifty yards below him on the slope—glanced up in sudden dismay.

The boulder struck an outcropping of rock and bounded almost lightly into the air, then came down heavily upon another upthrusting ledge farther down, shattering it. The outlaw seemed frozen in horror as this fearsome juggernaut thundered down the slope toward him, smiting into atoms whatever it found in its path.

The outlaw could have escaped. But he panicked. He turned to go in one direction and, in his haste, slipped on the treacherous gravel and talus littering the slope. Scrambling frantically back up onto his feet, he plunged wildly off in the opposite direction. Again he lost his footing. And then a third time.

Now Fargo saw mindless terror on the doomed man's face as he looked up and saw the onrushing boulder and its attendant avalanche. Smaller rocks, trees, and other debris, swept along ahead of the boulder, were bounding toward him now in an ever-widening swath of destruction. It must have seemed to him at that point that the entire slope was thundering down upon him.

The outlaw turned and cut diagonally down the slope. A small boulder, bounding ahead of the main avalanche, cut both his legs out from under him. He tried to scramble to his feet, but both legs were apparently shattered. Turning his head to look back, he saw the giant boulder overtaking him. He lifted one forearm in a futile gesture as the boulder took a graceful bound and came down squarely upon him—like a massive fist squashing a cockroach on a saloon bar.

Continuing on down the slope, the boulder thundered on across the canyon floor until, with a single, fearsome crunch, it smashed into the wall of rock opposite, breaking into three giant jagged chunks.

Fargo stood up, somewhat in awe of what he had accomplished with his back and an old branch. Farther down the slope, the dust and debris began to settle. A dark swath had been cut in the slope. Rivulets of loose sand and gravel still crawled toward the canyon floor and pebbles could be seen still bouncing on down the slope until finally even this activity was finished, and total silence blanketed the slope and the canyon below.

Fargo could just make out the outlaw lying on his back, spread-eagled. Reluctantly, he made his way down the slope until he reached the dead man. It was not a pleasant sight. Under the outlaw's body he found the man's Colt. There seemed to be no injury done to it. All it needed was a thorough cleaning. He dropped it into his holster and looked around for the dead man's hat, spotting it some distance farther down the slope. He went after it, whacked the dirt from it, then punched it back into shape and pulled it down gently over his throbbing head. It gave him almost immediate relief from the blistering sun.

Then he looked down into the canyon, searching for the outlaw's horse. It was in plain sight. The animal had bolted a quarter of a mile farther down the canyon and was now quietly cropping grass in a shady spot near the canyon wall.

Without a second glance at the outlaw's broken body, Fargo scrambled down the slope toward the horse.

4

The old prospector recognized Bart Mullin and his men instantly. Shoving his burro into the rock cleft, he squeezed in after him, ready to clobber the burro if it uttered a sound.

The three riders clattered past, doing their best to make their four mules hurry along. But old Sampson Riley could see that the mules were laboring under a fearsome load. The aparejos were close to ripping apart from their burden.

There was only one thing in the world took up that little space and still weighed that much. Gold!

At once Sampson knew what had happened. His eyes lit as he watched the three riders disappear behind a finger of rock and continue on into Diablo Canyon. Mullin's gang had finally raised the right stage, it looked like. And now they were stashing the gold bars in Diablo Canyon, more than likely in the abandoned mine. Sampson's smile grew broader. Nice of them to do that for him. Made his work a whole lot easier, it did.

The old prospector kept his eyes on the narrow

entrance to the canyon and listened as the sound of the gang's passage faded. At last the canyon was as still as death. The men were well inside by this time. It was safe for Sampson to move on.

He pulled his burro out of the cleft and stowed his pickax aboard the patient beast, took up the reins, and began leading him over the rocky ground at a steady pace. At seventy-three his once-proud six-foot-three frame had shrunken noticeably, but he knew he could still keep pace with an Apache brave and outlast any white man half his age.

As he hurried along, he wondered if Naratena knew what Bart Mullin and his gang of cutthroats were up to in Diablo Canyon. Then he chuckled hoarsely. Of course Naratena knew. There wasn't nothing that took place in this here sun-blasted wasteland without that redskin knowing about it.

Two hours later, astride the outlaw's big bay, Fargo caught sight of the prospector moving along the ridge below him, going in the opposite direction. Fargo decided he had best turn about and overtake him. He had finally lost the outlaw's trail on this hard, unyielding ground and needed help. Besides, this prospector below him just might have caught sight of Mullin and his gang, since he appeared to be returning from the same direction in which they had last been heading. At least, it was worth a try.

Fargo turned his horse, put it down the slope, and let it pick its way to the ridge below. Then he tapped his spurs to the animal's side and galloped after the prospector. The prospector saw him coming before he heard him, and pulled up to wait for Fargo to overtake him. He appeared edgy.

Fargo greeted him with a weary smile and slipped from his mount. The prospector was a bent man past seventy, but spare and hardy even so, wearing a ragged sombrero, a patched buckskin jacket, buckskin pants, and instead of boots, a pair of thigh-length Apache moccasins. His long beard was completely white, except for the chin, where tobacco juice had stained it a rich mahogany.

"Howdy," Fargo said, extending his hand. "Name's Fargo. Skye Fargo."

Sampson thrust out a gnarled hand and shook Fargo's. The grip was powerful and callused. "They calls me Sampson Riley. What be you doin' out here on a horse? This is burro country."

"And Apache country."

Sampson nodded quickly. "That, too."

"I'm looking for three men."

"That so?" Fargo saw a gleam in the old prospector's hazel eyes.

"Three men and four mules. The mules would be loaded down pretty heavy. They might even be lame by this time."

"Nope," the prospector said, shaking his head and letting loose a long yellow stream of tobacco juice. "They ain't lame. Not yet, they ain't."

"You seen 'em?"

"That's right. Who're you? How come you're trackin' them? You a sheriff or somethin'?"

"I was the shotgun messenger on the stage they raided. They killed one passenger and the jehu, Bill Gifford."

"Old Bill?" The prospector didn't like that. His face became hard with sudden resolve. "Now, that's a damn shame. Bill was always good for a smile and drink and slap on the back. Yessir, that's a shame."

"Where are they?"

"Don't knows I can tell you that right off."

"But you've seen them."

"Two hours ago. And then only for a minute. I kept out of sight, I did, and I was glad when they was gone."

"Where did you see them?"

"Diablo Canyon."

"Can you give me directions?"

Sampson Riley regarded Fargo shrewdly for a second or two, then shrugged. "Reckon I could do that."

The prospector went over to a sandy spot, found a stick, and began scratching out the outlines of canyons and streams. As he talked, identifying this stream and water hole, that rock formation or canyon, Fargo realized that this old man knew this country almost as well as did the Apaches.

When he had finished, Fargo straightened up and thanked him. But he straightened too quickly and almost lost his balance. He took a deep breath and steadied himself.

"What's the matter with you, mister?" Sampson said. "You ain't got no liquor on your breath, but you sure as hell don't stand very steady."

"Came down hard on my head when Mullin took the stage. It's been acting up pretty meanly."

"Cracked your skull, did you? Maybe you better

come with me to my cabin and rest up awhile. Goin' against that Mullin gang in your condition ain't such a good idea."

Fargo shook his head. "Thanks, Sampson. But I can't let them get too far ahead of me. I've had worse headaches than this, depending on the grade of whiskey."

The prospector shrugged. "Take care, then. You're big enough so you can, looks like."

Fargo moved back to his horse and pulled himself back onto his saddle. Then he glanced back at the prospector. "You got any idea what that gang'd be doing in that canyon?"

Sampson's eyes gleamed momentarily. Then he shook his head. "Hell, Fargo, why don't you go and find out? You should make it in a couple or three hours on the outside."

Waving good-bye, Fargo pulled his horse around.

Two hours later, still following the route Sampson had given him, Fargo found himself dry as a bone, having given the bay all the water that remained in his canteen. Sampson had mentioned a water hole near the canyon, slightly off the trail. Fargo found it with little difficulty and was pleased. This was a good sign. Sampson's directions, it seemed, could be trusted.

Dismounting carefully, Fargo slaked his thirst, then filled his canteen. It was gritty, red-tinged water, but he didn't complain. He filled his hat and allowed the horse to drink its full, then mounted up and kept going.

It was a couple of hours before sunset, a curious

chill having fallen over him, when he came within sight of the canyon Sampson had described. Looming out over the canyon's entrance were two great hornlike projections of rock—like the horns of a buffalo or, better yet, those of a devil. He had found Diablo Canyon. The entrance itself was narrow and twisting, the rock walls sheer and almost straight up.

Fargo rode back a ways, looking for a trail that might take him up onto the canyon's rim. He found it, a steep game trail that vanished in among ragged ledges and brush high above him. The difficult, gravelly terrain made it a difficult climb for the bay, and before Fargo reached the rim, he was forced to dismount and lead his horse the last fifty treacherous yards or so. Mounting up again, he followed the rim until he found at last what he was looking for: the wink of firelight on the floor of the canyon far below him.

Dismounting, he tied his bay up to a bristlecone pine and proceeded on foot along the rim of the canyon until he was almost directly above the campfire. He was on fire by this time, and he alternated between chills that turned his teeth into castanets and sudden, ravaging bouts of fever. He had almost gotten used to the rocking headache, but this new affliction left him weak and confused. It was difficult for him to relate it to his crack on the head.

It was not yet completely dark and Fargo could see the three remaining outlaws. One was squatting alongside the fire and the other two were reclining on their backs close by him, resting with their heads on their saddles. On the far side of the canyon, the three men had picketed their mounts. The mules were browsing near them, and the more closely Fargo peered at them, the more apparent it became that they were no longer carrying the load they had lugged into this canyon.

Somewhere in this canyon—and it appeared to Fargo that it might well go on forever—Mullin and his men had already cached the gold.

Hunkering down beside the campfire, Bart Mullin peered up nervously at the canyon rim. Clete had not caught up with them yet and he was beginning to worry. Could that damn shotgun messenger have survived, after all? Maybe he had blown Clete's fool head off. If Clete *had* bought it, that meant one less to split the raise with, and Mullin wasn't going to cry about that. On the other hand, what Clete had warned him about—that this damned shotgun messenger might follow them to this canyon and see where they stashed the gold—this did worry Mullin.

Mullin stood up and looked down at Tom and Lonny. They were lying on their backs near the campfire, using their saddles for pillows, letting the fire chase the desert chill that was already descending on them.

"Get up," he told them.

They stirred and glared up at him from under the brims of their hats.

"You heard me! Get the hell up!"

Grudgingly, the two men stood up.

"We're going up there on the slope, into those

shadows, and sleep there. Clete ain't come back. I'm expecting a visitor, maybe."

"Clete'll get here," drawled Lonny. "Give him a chance."

"I'm not arguing. We'll leave three dummy sleepers here wrapped in blankets and sleep up on the slope. Now move it!"

The grumbling went on during the entire operation, but Mullin paid no heed as long as they moved quickly and did what they were told. When, about a half-hour later, he and the other two were spotted at different locations on the slope, he began to feel better. Lonny was to his left, a little below him, and Tom was above him to his right. The campfire was about thirty yards below them, and in the light of the still-bright campfire, he could see clearly the blanket-wrapped dummies "sleeping" around it.

He glanced up. The western rim of the canyon was almost directly overhead. The moon was behind it, invisible to his eyes, but he could see its bright wash on the canyon wall opposite. He leaned back against his saddle, took out his six-gun, and waited.

Fargo had watched the entire operation with great interest. It had been a clever move on the part of the gang leader, and it meant that Bart Mullin was aware of the likelihood that Fargo might very well be on his trail. Fargo's problem now, apart from his appalling weakness, was how to get all three men close enough to take them. He could wait until the morning, perhaps, and surprise them while they were riding out, but there was no assurance that they would be riding close enough together for him to be able to take all three.

No. He had to act now, under cover of darkness. And while he was still capable of action. Teeth chattering like castanets, he peered down at the fire, his mind racing.

At last he got to his feet and started down the steep slope to the canyon floor. It was a long, difficult descent and Fargo was so painstaking that he did not allow himself to put all his weight on a rock or a section of ground until he had tested it thoroughly to make sure it was stable. When at last he reached the canyon floor, the moon was bright overhead, with the three outlaws still cloaked in darkness under the canyon's western rim. Fortunately, the moon had shifted enough so that the campfire, still glowing brightly in the darkness, was also in shadow.

Fargo took four cartridges out of the gun belt he had taken from Clete and tossed them underhand into the fire. He heard them land and saw two small geysers of sparks, indicating that two of the cartridges had landed in the glowing bed of coals. He tossed two more and saw one land in the fire. That would have to do it, Fargo realized, crouching behind a boulder. He rested his revolver on the top of the boulder to steady it, and waited.

For a while he thought the fire was not going to be hot enough to detonate the cartridges. Then the first one detonated. After that came the second one. Fargo watched the slope. From far off came a startled cry and then a muzzle flash as one of the outlaws fired down in the direction of the campfire.

Swiftly, Fargo aimed at a spot just above the flash and returned his fire. He heard a cry and the distant sound of something metallic striking the ground.

A moment later, the second cartridge detonated, followed by another gun flash much lower on the slope. Again Fargo used the muzzle flash for a target and fired rapidly at the spot, spreading his fire carefully. After this came answering fire, directed at the boulder behind which Fargo crouched. This was what Fargo had been hoping for, since it enabled him to pinpoint more accurately where this second outlaw was. As the outlaw's rounds ricocheted off the boulder in front of him, he aimed carefully and fired twice more, emptying his gun. The sound of another cry rent the night as this gunman, too, was hit.

Fargo had no way of knowing how severely he had wounded the two men, and he had not drawn fire from the third outlaw, who remained hidden on the slope. This third outlaw was probably Mullin himself. The outlaw chief was too smart to fall for Fargo's trick, it seemed.

Fargo turned to the task of reloading his revolver. But by this time his hands were shaking so much that, even though the moon had moved enough so that it was shining directly down on him, he still could not seem to get his fingers to cooperate with his eyes. It was not only his blinding headache, but also the chills that now racked his body almost continuously.

Still, doggedly, like one slipping into a dream, he persisted in attempting to drop the cartridges into the cylinders, even though it was now obvious to him that it had become an impossible feat.

But he was simply too far gone.

Out of the shadows stepped Bart Mullin, a tall, horse-faced man with protruding teeth, and eyes that regarded Fargo with cool interest. His six-gun was trained on Fargo.

Shaking his head blearily, Fargo tried to raise his own weapon, forgetting that he had not yet succeeded in loading it. But the revolver seemed to weigh a ton.

"Who the hell are you?" he heard Bart Mullin ask him.

Fargo was too weary to reply.

"You're that shotgun messenger took Rex Barry's place. The one called Fargo."

"Give that man a cigar," Fargo muttered, dropping his empty gun and falling forward to lean on the boulder.

Mullin stepped closer, his eyes narrowing. "What about Clete? Did you kill him?"

Before Fargo could reply, Mullin answered his own question by striding forward and whipping the hat off Fargo's head.

"Well, well! This here's Clete's hat," he said, chuckling. "Looks like you did it, mister. You kept me from having to share any of that gold. I guess maybe I owe you."

As he said this, he swung his six-gun and caught Fargo on the side of his face. Fargo toppled to the ground, landing on his side. He looked up past Mullin, and it seemed to him that the canyon walls were beginning to spin about them both. He reached his hands out to hang on.

Mullin cocked his six-gun and aimed carefully down at Fargo's head. Fargo closed his eyes and waited. He was too sick, too tired to protest. The cold stony ground upon which he rested seemed to cradle him almost gently.

But instead of the crashing detonation of Mullin's six-gun, Fargo heard the man's sudden gasp. A second later came the sound of his six-gun clattering to the ground.

Fargo opened his eyes. Mullin was standing with his legs apart, both hands clasped about the shaft of an arrow embedded in his chest. The outlaw was straining mightily on the shaft in a futile attempt to pull it out, a look of defiant fury on his face. He sank to his knees and was still trying to pull the shaft from his chest when he toppled to one side and vanished back into the canyon's shadow.

Fargo was sorry Mullin had not been able to get off his shot. A bullet would have given him a quicker death than that granted by the inventive mind of an Apache warrior.

Fargo heard the soft pattering sound of moccasined feet surrounding him. He felt himself lifted by small, strong hands. His eyes opened. He was looking up into the face of an Apache warrior. The Indian's dark, savage face was impassive, his anthracite eyes revealing nothing of his intentions. The face vanished as the Indian stepped back. Abruptly, Fargo felt himself thrown over an Indian's broad, powerful shoulder. He was dimly aware of other Apaches on either side of him.

The Apaches began to run with the seemingly effortless ease typical of the Apache warrior. Fargo closed his eyes. All he could hope for now was that he would be dead before they reached the Apache encampment.

5

In one of the many nightmares that followed, Fargo found himself once again with his father.

He was walking along a crowded sidewalk with him when he caught sight of a drayman flogging his horse unmercifully. The poor laboring brute was attempting frantically to haul a load of whiskey barrels out of a deep mud hole. As the drayman's slashing whip sank into the animal's quivering flanks, the horse's eyes started from its head in terror, its muzzle laced with lather. Unable to stand the sight, Fargo had broken away from his father and darted out into the street to plead with the drayman.

But the drayman would not listen. He flung out his arm and knocked the young Fargo into the mud, then continued his merciless lashing of the horse. Crying out in horror, Fargo jumped up and attempted to wrest the whip from the drayman's hands. Again he failed. But by this time his father had joined him, and soon other bystanders were swarming out into the street to aid his father.

The whip was snatched from the drayman's hand and Fargo's father knocked the fellow to the ground, after which the crowd of onlookers placed their backs to the wagon and pushed it out of the hole.

Only then did Fargo's father and the others allow the drayman to drive off.

Afterward, Fargo's father smiled proudly down at his son. "There's only one thing worse than a man who would beat a horse," he said, "and that's someone who would stand by and let it happen."

But even as his father said this, his kindly face vanished. Darkness descended on him and Fargo heard cries of lamentation. Black-garbed figures bent close to him. It was raining. A crowd of bent figures stood before twin coffins. A desolation filled his soul. He turned and ran and found himself back in town, racing down a familiar alley, calling out for his father and his mother.

Hands reached out to hold him, but he shook them off. He struggled and cried out. Tears streamed down his face—only it was not the townsman holding him now, but a pack of howling Indians, their faces painted hideously. He screamed and tried to free himself, but powerful arms lifted him. He felt himself being borne aloft and carried toward a hellish landscape of fire and brimstone . . .

There were other nightmares—peopled by a host

of fiendishly resourceful devils who forced evil-tasting brews down his throat, or kept him imprisoned in the smoke-filled wickiup while they sucked on long-stemmed ceremonial pipes and sang in a high, maddening singsong, the strong, acrid smoke from their pipes reaching deep into his lungs.

More than once—though he was never sure if this was a dream or reality—Fargo arose from his bed of pine boughs and filthy blankets and went forth into a dim, twilit world crowded with grotesque scenes and half-naked Apache warriors who danced like possessed painted dolls before his fevered vision.

At other times Fargo found himself sitting across from a medicine man squatting cross-legged before him. The Indian's small, nut-brown face was a spiderweb of wrinkles. His white hair, light and feathery, lifted constantly in the hot wind that blew in through the wickiup's open flap.

He came usually when Fargo's brain seemed to have expanded to a size that could no longer be contained within the confines of his skull. At such times, Fargo wanted only to rip open his skull so as to free himself from the crushing, blinding pain that seethed, trapped, within it. The old Indian would enter his wickiup chanting. As he sat before Fargo, he would continue chanting in a high, quavering wail, his open mouth revealing the black stumps of his few remaining teeth. All the while he chanted, he reached over continually to place his palsied hands gently on Fargo's head—until gradually, the intense pain would recede and Fargo could feel himself tumbling backward into a blessed, painless sleep.

The last time the Indian medicine man visited Fargo in his wickiup, he finished his chant by extending to Fargo the pipe he was smoking. When Fargo tried to refuse it, others came to hold Fargo down. The medicine man's face drew closer, while his stump-toothed smile seemed to fill the dark interior of the wickiup . . .

Whether it was the same dream or another, Fargo was not certain, but he found himself on the side of a mountain or canyon. It was night. A bonfire was sending tongues of flame high enough to scorch the moon.

Fargo himself was dancing around the fire with the Apaches, his tall, powerful frame towering over the smaller, more blockily built savages. The sweat on their powerful brown bodies gleamed in the light from the fire, and a fever of excitement surged through Fargo's limbs, galvanizing him, causing him to shout with the others, to join with them in their pagan dance, to fling back his head and cry out to White Painted Woman and her son, Child of Water.

In his madness he flung himself against a huge boulder, the Apaches at his side urging him on, their painted faces close to his, their eyes wild. Straining mightily, he found himself back on that other slope, the outlaw Clete scrambling up toward him. Once again he felt a thick branch in his grasp as he thrust the end of it under the boulder, while a host of smaller, but equally powerful bodies joined his in inching the immense boulder to the lip of the ledge. He felt the ground under the mighty boulder groan, then it rose slightly. With a crunching, ominous thump, the boulder dipped from sight and began rolling ponderously down the steep slope, disappearing almost at once into the darkness.

It felt as if the entire mountain had shifted under his feet. The air was filled with debris. Heavy clouds of dirt swirled about his head, obliterating the leaping flames from the many fires kindled all about him. He felt hands pulling at him and once again he was looking into wild, painted faces, the drums throbbing even more insistently now, the night spinning wildly about him until the moon and the stars swung out of their orbits and he felt himself falling, falling . . .

When at last Fargo emerged from this strange, disordered world of sick visions and even wilder dreams, he was taken out of the wickiup and allowed to sit in the warm sun for days. Gradually, his senses returned. Now when he slept, the nightmares did not come. The pain in his skull had abated almost completely and his vision was no longer impaired. The Apache women fed him and brought him water, but did not offer themselves to him.

At last, late one day, an Indian pony was brought to him—along with the rest of his gear, including his Colt and hat. An Apache brave indicated he should mount up. Fargo was surprised, but pleased. He was going to be able to ride out.

As he mounted up and sat back in the saddle, he

looked around him at the mean wickiups, their brush sides patched with army blankets. The squaws and children, along with the other braves, stood back and watched him impassively with a silent respect Fargo could not understand. They should have killed him long ago. Why had they not done so?

The chief, a long-nosed, fierce-looking Apache with surprising blue eyes, approached and mounted alongside Fargo, two other warriors mounting their ponies behind him. Without a word the Apache took out a black bandanna, leaned over, and tied it around Fargo's head, effectively blindfolding him. Other Apaches stepped forward then and bound both of his wrists securely to the saddle horn, after which his feet were bound to the stirrups.

One of the Apaches took the reins of his pony and they rode off.

Through the rest of that day they kept on, traveling through the night, dismounting only twice during that time. When Fargo felt at last the first faint rays of the morning sun on his face, his blindfold was taken from his eyes and his Indian escort wheeled their ponies and galloped off without a word.

Blinking painfully in the bright morning light, Fargo saw that his horse was heading toward a small adobe cabin and barn on a long flat less than a quarter of a mile away. The two buildings were nestled in under four cottonwoods, the only tall vegetation his eye could find in any direction. When he got closer, he saw a thin trickle of a stream almost lost in the gravelly, rock-littered water-course behind the cabin. Fargo managed to pull his hands free of the saddle horn, but his attempts to get at his bound feet were futile. At last he was able to lean far enough forward to grab first the bridle, then the reins of his horse.

When he had ridden to within a hundred yards or so of the cabin, a rifle cracked, the detonation shattering the early-morning stillness. Fargo immediately pulled up, aware that the shot had been meant as a warning to ride no closer. He waited patiently until the same old prospector he had met earlier emerged from a clump of rocks beside the cabin. He was carrying a rifle. Out from behind him came a young woman, her corn-silk hair gleaming in the morning sunlight. She also was carrying a rifle.

As Fargo nudged his horse closer, the girl shaded her eyes with her hand. The prospector said something to her, then started across the rocky ground to meet Fargo. By the time he reached Fargo, he was smiling. "Looks like we already met, Fargo."

"Do you usually shoot at approaching strangers?"

"Them's the only kind I worry about. It's a habit I got into—a good one. Nothin' personal, mind you."

"Help me get out of these stirrups, will you?"

The prospector took out his hunting knife and slashed the rawhide that bound Fargo's feet. Fargo dismounted, and the two men started toward the cabin, Fargo leading the Indian pony.

"So you're the One Who Moves Mountains, eh?" the prospector said.

"What the hell do you mean by that?"

The prospector shrugged. "All I know is that's what Naratena calls you. There's fresh coffee in the cabin—and a bed, if you're weary. You're welcome to stay with me, if you want. 'Less'n you want to go back to an Apache wickiup."

"For now, I'll take your offer, and thanks."

They pulled up in front of the girl.

"Carrie, this is Skye Fargo, a gent I met some time ago. He asked me the way to Diablo Canyon and I told him." Then he grinned. "Never thought I'd see him again."

Fargo nodded to the young woman. She appraised him coolly, but not without interest. "Pleased to meet you," she said, her voice like a caress.

The girl could not have been more than twenty. In addition to the straw-colored hair, she had dark, almost violet eyes, a light skin tanned golden from the sun, lips that appeared to have just tasted strawberries, high cheekbones, and a strong, assertive chin. She was wearing a simple, pale shift of a dress that did little to hide the ripeness of her young body. As he contemplated her, Fargo felt desire—naked and unashamed—stir to life within him once again.

In that instant, he knew he was well again.

"I'll take your horse," Carrie told him.

He handed her the reins and followed the prospector inside the cabin. Thanks to its thick adobe walls, the interior was blessedly cool. It was also surprisingly large. The kitchen and living room consisted of one long room, with two large bedrooms, one leading off the living room, the other off the kitchen. The ceilings were beams made from old mine timbers, and the same material was used to frame the door and windows.

Fargo was impressed.

Sampson saw the look on Fargo's face and chuckled. "No reason to live like an Apache if you don't have to."

"And I guess you don't have to."

Sampson did not bother to reply as he joined Fargo at the table. After a moment, he shook his head in mild amazement. "Like I said before, Fargo, I never thought I'd ever lay eyes on you again—not after I sent you into that canyon after Mullin and his gang."

"You didn't think I could handle them."

"I did not. You looked like the wrath of God, that you did. I was surprised you were able to stay on your horse."

"I wasn't feeling very healthy at that," Fargo admitted. He took a deep breath and leaned back in his chair. "I'm beginning to understand," he went on. "Naratena left me off here so I'd find your place."

"Yes."

"How come?"

Sampson shrugged. "About six months ago Naratena sent Carrie the same way," he said. "Later on he told me she had been taken from a band of *rurales* who'd treated her . . . poorly—so poorly she was half out of her mind. Her queer

67

behavior frightened the Apaches. You know how they regard anyone who's tetched."

Fargo nodded. Perhaps for a while he had appeared the same way to Naratena's band. "Carrie looks okay now," Fargo said.

"Ah, yes," Sampson said proudly. "She does that."

They heard Carrie's footsteps approaching the door and went silent. Fargo turned and watched as the girl entered. Immediately, she set about preparing their coffee. She seemed as pleased and excited at Fargo's unexpected presence as he was to find such a beautiful girl out here in the middle of nowhere. Their eyes kept catching each other's. Something alive and vital had already sprung up between them. Fargo wondered at the relationship between Sampson and the girl. The prospector was old, but surely not so old he could live this close to such lush ripeness without at least tasting of it.

He watched her as she placed the cups in front of them and then poured out the steaming black coffee. When she handed him a small earthen cup containing honey for his coffee, he thanked her, then forced himself to look away from her.

"What day is this?" he asked Sampson. "I lost track of time while I was with them Apaches."

"This here's a Friday."

Fargo frowned. "That makes it almost a week since I left Gold City."

Sampson Riley laughed. "Think again."

"You mean two weeks?"

"Three would be more like it."

"I guess I was sicker than I thought."

68

"You damn well were."

"How come the Apaches took care of me like that?"

"That was Naratena's doing. Seems he took a liking to you. He'd been watchin' your exploits since you took after Mullin and his gang."

Fargo thought a minute, then looked with sudden sharpness at Sampson. "That's what you meant, then—that business about the One Who Moves Mountains. Naratena must've seen me roll that boulder down on one of Mullin's gang."

"I guess that's it, if that's what you done."

"I had no choice."

"But that ain't the only reason he thinks your medicine is so powerful."

"What's the other reason?"

"You drank from a water hole he had poisoned, and according to him and the other Apaches, it had little or no effect on you."

Fargo swore softly. That water hole had been poisoned! No wonder he had felt so rotten. And then he thought of the bay he had left behind when he went after Mullin and his men. It was not a pleasant thought.

Sampson shook his head in wonderment. "You drank up and just kept right on and tracked Mullin's gang to Diablo Canyon, then killed two more of his men. Naratena said you had Mullin braced when he and his Apaches took a hand in things."

"Hell! I didn't have him braced," Fargo protested. "Mullin had me down. I was waiting for his bullet. By then that Apache devil's poison was rais-

69

ing hell with me. I was in no condition to fight back—and now I know why."

"It wasn't you they was after when they poisoned that water hole. It was Mullin and his men. The Apaches sure didn't like Mullin. But you they liked. Or at least, you they respected. One thing an Apache honors, and that's a brave man— even a brave white eyes. I was at their camp a couple of times while you were there. From what I could see, you was keeping that old Zuni medicine man pretty damn busy."

Fargo leaned back in his chair. An image of that old Indian's prunelike face appeared before his mind's eye. "You say that was a Zuni medicine man takin' care of me?"

"Yep. Naratena's people captured him a long time ago."

Fargo understood now. This, then, was one reason why he had survived. Throughout the Southwest it was common knowledge that the Zuni medicine men were the wisest and most skillful of all when it came to healing, which was why they were so often abducted by other tribes. Fargo did not know what magic this old Zuni had used on him, but whatever it was, it had saved Fargo's life.

Fargo looked at Sampson with renewed interest. "You deal with the Apaches pretty regular, it looks like."

"I deal with them. Yes."

"How come?"

"Survival. This is their country. Not mine."

"There's others who'd disagree with that. Like

those miners in Gold City itchin' to get into these mountains."

Sampson shrugged.

Fargo glanced once more around the cabin. Everywhere he looked he saw evidence of prosperity. Fine cooking utensils, rugs on the floor as well as colorful tapestries on the walls. Even curtains at the window. Sampson seemed to lack for nothing.

Peering back at Sampson, he said, "You've made a deal with these Apaches, I figure. They let you pan for gold in return for something. It would have to be pretty valuable for them to let you do that."

Sampson smiled. "It is that. It's gold I give them. They let me pan the streams in these mountains— one stream in particular near Diablo Canyon. I give them half of what I take out, and they let me keep the other half for my trouble. Panning for gold is squaws' work, so they are perfectly willin' to let me grub for them."

"What do the Apaches want gold for?"

"To buy rifles from the Comancheros."

Fargo frowned. He didn't know if he liked that idea. "I see," he said, leaning back in his chair, eyeing Sampson speculatively.

"Mebbe you do, mebbe you don't. You can hate the Apaches or you can like 'em, but you sure as hell can't ignore 'em. One way or another they'll get the rifles they need. This is their land, don't forget. I figure if they get the rifles this way, it'll cost a lot fewer burned cabins and dead prospectors."

Fargo could not deny the truth of that. For decades, Indians—the Apache, especially—had been purchasing from the Comancheros rifles and ammunition as well as box after box of steel arrowheads. That the Apaches were now using freshly panned gold dust provided by Sampson changed nothing really. And as Sampson pointed out, it undoubtedly prevented the Apaches from raiding homesteads and killing still more prospectors for the wherewhithal they needed for this trade. In a way, Fargo supposed, Sampson was saving lives.

"Maybe you got a point, at that, Sampson. But hell, Naratena's poison almost killed me."

Sampson shook his head. "That ain't the full truth. It wasn't only the poison laid you low. Your skull was cracked open like an eggshell. I heard the Zuni tell Naratena. That's where most of your trouble was. How'd that happen? Do you remember?"

"It could've been when I fell from the stage. I came down pretty hard on the back of my head."

Carrie was sitting across from Fargo. She had been listening intently. "How does it feel now?" she asked.

With a grin, Fargo took off his hat and felt it gingerly. "Tender, but it's all in one piece."

"From what I hear," Sampson said, "that sure as hell ain't the way it was when they brought you into the Apache camp."

This unequivocal assertion caused Fargo to lean back in his chair and think back on the events leading up to his capture by the Apaches. Now that he thought of it, his head *had* been aching something fierce—even to the point of affecting his vision.

And most of the time during his stay in that Apache wickiup, he had been out of his head entirely, filled with visions of the past and wild, chaotic dreams. A fractured skull could do such things to a man—and worse. It could kill him. Remembering others Fargo had seen over the years who had suffered such a head injury—and how in some cases it had left them—Fargo shuddered. "Guess I'm lucky, at that."

Sampson nodded.

"Which means I owe Naratena."

"Yep. Even though he's a half-naked savage who ain't even Christian. You owe him."

Fargo smiled his agreement. "You see this black hair of mine? It's a gift from my mother. She was more Indian than white, and proud of it. So am I."

Sampson smiled. "Now, tell me," he said, "what did you see when you tracked Mullin into Diablo Canyon?"

"You mean, did I see where Mullin cached all that gold?"

Sampson leaned forward in his seat, his eyes gleaming. "That's right. Did you?"

"By the time I overtook them, they had already hidden the gold somewhere."

"Somewhere in Diablo Canyon, you mean?"

"That's what I mean."

"But you don't know where."

"I'll find it."

"You think so, do you?"

"I do. I'm going back to Gold City and get the express agent and the sheriff out here—and whoever else is willing to come. We're going to scour that canyon and find that gold."

"You take your obligations serious, do you, now?"

Fargo looked grimly at Sampson. "I was hired to keep that gold safe, and I ain't about to let Wells Fargo down. My pa was a Wells Fargo agent. That's why I call myself Fargo."

Sampson leaned back in his seat, his eyebrows moving up a notch. "Well, now, I guess a man can't put it any clearer than that."

Despite the coffee, Fargo felt a sudden, overwhelming fatigue. His limbs had became leaden. Recalling the long night he had spent in the saddle, he did not wonder at it. Now that he was in this cool adobe cabin, he found himself looking forward with a kind of childish craving to a bed off the floor and clean blankets.

"Mr. Fargo," Carrie said, "you look like you're ready to drop."

"Guess maybe I am," admitted Fargo, smiling wearily at the girl. "I rode all night and part of the day before."

Carrie looked at Sampson. "He can sleep in my bed," she told him.

"Good idea. It's the coolest room."

Fargo pushed himself erect and felt himself stagger slightly. He grinned apologetically. At once Carrie got to her feet and took his arm while Sampson hurried on ahead of them into her bedroom and pulled back the sheets on her bed.

Fargo dimly remembered sprawling facedown on the bed, Carrie's swift, fingers stripping him, then the feel of the light sheet covering him.

He slept as he had not slept in a long, long time.

6

Fargo awoke the next day, brilliant sunshine pouring into the bedroom. He stirred and sat up just as the bedroom door opened and Carrie appeared in the doorway, smiling at him. Now he knew what had awakened him. The smell of bacon and eggs and coffee that swept into the room the moment Carrie opened the door.

"Are you hungry?" she asked.

"I could eat a horse. A big one."

"Get dressed," she replied, smiling. "But all I have is bacon and eggs and coffee, and some home-made bread."

Then she pulled the door shut so he could get dressed, and when he appeared a moment later, his britches and boots on, his chest bare, she had already set the table for him. He was, it appeared, to be the only one at the table.

"Where's Sampson?" he asked, sitting down.

"He rode out early with Naratena, I think. He'll be gone for some time. He usually is when he goes off with Naratena."

"He and that Apache are pretty thick," commented Fargo, taking up his knife and fork and attacking his breakfast.

Carrie sat down opposite him. "Yes," she said, watching his face closely. "He is. And I should think you would be, too. Naratena saved your life, don't forget."

"I'll not forget, but it seems the only thing I heard in Gold City were disputes concerning the Apaches. Not about the need to exterminate them—but how soon to go about it. There was talk of arousing a posse and cleaning the Apaches out of these mountains—and soon. And at one saloon, the patrons were circulating a petition asking for the army to march in and take care of what they called the Apache Problem."

"I can imagine."

"They got a point, you know. Any prospector tries to get into these mountains for the gold they know is in here either disappears or staggers back with his hide stuck like a pincushion."

"Then they should stay out. This is Apache country."

"Maybe it is for now. But that won't last, I'm thinking."

She dropped her eyes. "Yes," she agreed unhappily. "I'm afraid you're right. So now you see why Sampson is helping Naratena purchase the weapons he and his people need to defend their land."

"I heard you was from Texas."

"I was. And I'm headin' back as soon as I can."

"I don't blame you. That's pretty country. But you sure don't sound like a Texan—talking about the Apaches in that fashion."

"We live and learn, Mr. Fargo."

He grinned at her and lifted his coffee. "Some of us do, anyway."

She returned his smile. "How was your breakfast?"

"What do you think?"

"From the way you attacked it, I'd say it was a success."

"What else do you have?"

"You mean you're still hungry?"

"I mean, to drink."

She laughed softly and hastened over to a cupboard under the sink. Opening it, she produced a gallon earthenware jug and brought it and a tin cup over to the table. Setting both down before him, she said, "I'll let you pour."

"What is it?"

"Mescal."

"Won't you join me?"

"I'd rather not. I've already tasted it, thank you."

Fargo unstoppered the jug, filled the cup, and tossed the liquor down. The mescal set off a conflagration that singed his tonsils, then burned a fiery path all the way to his stomach. In a few moments his toes were tingling and small beads of perspiration were standing out on his forehead.

With wide, appreciative eyes, he poured himself another drink. "Best mescal I've tasted in a coon's age."

"A present to Sampson from Naratena."

"The real article—no doubt about it."

As he lifted the cup to his lips, she reached over and gently took his hand. "Isn't that supposed to make a man . . . well, you know."

He saw her meaning at once. She was wrong, of course. A good powerful brew had never slowed him.

But her question had made it damn clear what she had in mind, and he figured there was no sense at all in wasting any more time. He put down his drink and got to his feet. She smiled up at him. He went around to her and, taking both of her hands in his, gently pulled her up out of her chair. Then he lifted her easily into his arms. She laughed, delighted, and with her eyes alight with excitement, encircled his neck with her arms and kissed him warmly, hungrily, on the lips.

Turning, he carried her back into the bedroom. They struck the bed together and in a steaming fury of impatience soon stripped each other bare. Fargo's big hand grabbed her buttocks and swept her hungrily under him. Opening her thighs wide, Carrie reached up and hugged him to her as he plunged deep into her.

Jesus, Fargo thought, feeling her hot flesh engulf him. It had been so long, he had almost forgotten how good it felt.

An obliterating totality of desire overwhelmed him as he devoured her lips and began thrusting with a hungry, brutal abandon. Thought, volition, design, were all absent. He felt now only desire and her powerful, moaning thrusting warmth as she answered him stroke for stroke, building like him to a powerful and shattering climax. When it came, he cried out, while she, laughing and bucking under him, let out a long, low moan.

It was over almost as quickly as it had begun. They had been like two kids stripping and plunging into a water hole in the middle of a blistering summer day. The shock of it, the need for it, had taken over completely. They lay in each other's arms for a long while, thinking about it.

"Mmm," she said at length. "I guess that mescal didn't hurt you any."

He stroked her long golden hair. "I'm not finished," he told her.

She laughed softly, seductively. "I know," she said. "I can feel you still in there, Mr. Fargo. There's so *much* of you."

"I hope you ain't complaining."

"What do you think?"

As she spoke, she pushed him over onto his back and mounted him, plunging down upon him with a recklessness that almost made him wince. Then she flung her head back and began moving. It was a revelation. He felt the flame kindling once again deep within his groin.

"Oh," she said, "that feels so *good*."

Fargo was too busy for comment.

Suddenly, her face scarlet and shiny with perspiration, she leaned forward, swinging her nipples across Fargo's face.

"Suck them!" she cried. "Oh, please, suck them!"

He did as she suggested while her long blond

hair enclosed him in a lovely, scented tent. She cried out in ecstasy and began quivering violently. Afraid that she was going to lose control, Fargo reached up with both hands and grabbed her about the hipbones, driving her with brutal force back down onto him.

She caught his rhythm then and they began thrusting in unison. At once he felt himself rising to his second climax. Before long, in perfect unison, they were locked together in each other's embrace, his face buried in her breasts, her body arched over him. At last, his hands still frozen onto her thighs, he came in a screaming, panting explosion.

A second later, she came as well.

"Oh, Jesus, Fargo," she cried, throwing herself forward onto him, her arms sweeping his head up into the hollow of her breast. "I can't stop."

And that's what it felt like as he clutched her to him and felt her shuddering upon him again and again—in what appeared to be a series of violent, internal explosions.

Light-headed and fully dressed, feeling satisfyingly empty, Fargo watched Carrie, back in her rough but exciting shift, carefully pour herself a cup of mescal. They were back at the kitchen table. Downing his own drink quickly—the same one he had left on the table—he grinned at her, daring her to do the same.

She raised one eyebrow, took one sip of the mescal, and another, then tossed the rest of it down her throat. Shuddering, she wiped her mouth as tears sprang into the corners of her eyes.

"Whee! I really didn't need that," she exclaimed, blowing her breath out and waving her hand. "What we just had was as good as any liquor."

"Better," he agreed, "but there's no sense in letting good native mescal go to waste."

"If you say so."

They sat for a while in silence, content just to be together in the cool kitchen, remembering. Then, Fargo stirred himself and smiled at Carrie.

"Carrie," he said, "a little while ago you mentioned something about going back to Texas as soon as you can. Did you mean that?"

She nodded. "I got folks back there. They probably think I'm dead now—and I guess I would've been if Naratena hadn't taken me from those *rurales*."

"How come the Apaches let you go?"

She smiled wanly. "I was half-crazy by the time they got me. And that made me pretty useless to them. So when Sampson expressed an interest in me, Naratena let Sampson take me with him."

"When you return to Texas, will you go back with Sampson?"

She smiled sadly. "No. This is his home. He wouldn't leave these mountains."

"But I thought you and him—"

She shrugged sadly, catching his drift instantly. "That would have been very nice. And I really think I would have liked that. But Sampson insists that at his age he's not up to it. You know what I mean, of course. And I just couldn't convince him that it really didn't matter to me. But I guess it sure

81

does matter to him. You men and your foolish pride."

"Maybe it's pride, Carrie, and maybe it's just good sense. I've seen old men trying to hang on to younger women. They can do it for a while, but only for a while."

"I suppose you're right." She grinned mischievously at him. "Just now in there with you I realized how much I needed all a man can give me—and maybe even just a little more." She leaned over and kissed him lightly on the cheek.

Chuckling, Fargo poured himself another cup of the mescal. As he was doing so, he heard a horse approaching the cabin. Carrie jumped up, ran to the door, and flung it open. Fargo heard Carrie greet Sampson, and a moment later Sampson stomped through the door and into the cabin, Carrie following in after him. He took one look at Fargo and at the jug in front of him and smiled broadly.

"You look healthy enough," Sampson said, taking off his hat and hanging it on a hook by the door.

"Thanks. I'm feeling a whole lot better. Thanks to you and Carrie. Join me in a drink. This here is fine mescal."

"Naratena's best. Don't mind if I do."

Sampson slumped down at the table and took the jug from Fargo. Carrie put a cup down before him, but he ignored it. Lifting the jug to his shoulder, he leaned his head back and took the mescal straight from the jug, swallowing the liquid fire in a series of prodigious gulps. Finished, he thumped the jug back onto the table and wiped his mouth.

"Good for worms," he said. Then he cocked his head and studied Fargo for a moment. "Well, now, Mr. Fargo," he said, "you look fit enough to wrassle bears. What are your plans? You still itchin' to go bring that gold out of Diablo Canyon?"

"Yes."

"What'll you be tellin' that Wells Fargo agent, Bridger?"

"I'll tell Bridger just what happened."

"That Mullin and his gang buried the gold in Diablo Canyon."

"Yes," Fargo said.

"And then you're bringing him and whoever else you can back in here with you to find it."

"That's my plan."

"You realize the Apaches won't like that."

"That gold is Wells Fargo property."

"Yes. You told me how you felt about that. I understand. So you want to return that gold to Wells Fargo."

"I like to finish what I start."

Sampson leaned back in his chair. Fargo could tell the old man was mentally reordering a host of priorities as he stroked his tobacco-stained beard.

"Then maybe I got some good news for you," he told Fargo abruptly. "Naratena's gone south for a war council with Victorio."

"You mean his Apaches are going to join up with Victorio?"

"I doubt it. It's just a parley. But while he's gone, we could maybe sneak into that canyon and—"

"We?"

"You'll need my help to find Diablo Canyon again."

"I found it once. I can find it again."

Sampson shook his head. "Think back. Can you remember that map I made for you in the dust?"

The Trailsman thought a moment, then shook his head.

"And how many landmarks do you remember on your way to the canyon?"

The old prospector had a point. The events of that day were but a dim, feverish memory now. Trying to recall the trail he had followed on his way to Diablo Canyon was worse than trying to recall a disordered dream.

"Not a one," admitted Fargo ruefully. "So it looks like I'll be needing your help to find the canyon."

"Not only the canyon. You'll need my help to find the gold. You told me when you got there, the gold was gone—stashed somewhere."

"That's right."

"Did you see where?"

"No, I didn't. But, like I told you before, we'll just have to scour that canyon until we find that gold."

Sampson chuckled. "You got any idea how long that canyon is?"

Fargo shook his head.

"Close to thirty miles."

Fargo sat back and frowned. "Shit," he said.

"And you don't have no idea where it could be hid."

"No, I don't."

The old man grinned. "Well, I do. There's an abandoned mine in a box canyon branching off Diablo Canyon. It's in pretty far, but my hunch is that's where we'll find the gold."

"Sounds reasonable."

"And you can take my word for it, Fargo. Without my help, finding that box canyon won't be easy. There are hundreds of other, smaller canyons and arroyos branchin' off Diablo, and each one's swallowed up its share of prospectors. I reckon I'm about the only one knows that canyon well enough to guide you to it again—aside from the Apaches, of course."

Fargo smiled at the old man. "All right. I'll take your word for it. And I'd think maybe I'd prefer you take us in there, not the Apaches."

"You realize I ain't doin' this for nothing. I figure Wells Fargo is rich enough to give me a reward."

"A reward?"

The old man's eyes gleamed. "That's right. A percentage of the gold's value. You could speak to Bridger for me. Tell him without my help that gold is lost in there forever. And if they wait too long, Naratena will be back and there'll be no chance any of them will be able to get into that canyon and out of it again—alive."

"I'll tell him. I don't see he'll have any choice but to go along."

"Maybe—but there's just one thing in all this I don't like."

"What's that?"

Sampson shook his head unhappily. "We'll be dealing with Bridger. I don't trust him. He's an ex-preacher, you know. And once them fellers fall off the wagon, they usually get so low down, they have to look up to find a snake's belly."

"I don't like Bridger, either. But he's the Wells Fargo agent."

"We'll just have to keep an eye on him, then. It's a chance we'll have to take." The old prospector glanced with sudden warmth at Carrie. "But it's a chance I'm willin' to take. Carrie's goin' back to Texas when all this is over, and I want her to have somethin' for what she's been through."

"Now, Sampson," Carrie cried, "there's no need for that. You've already done enough for me."

"Carrie, you let me be the judge of that," he said, taking her hand. "You're the granddaughter I never had. Just let me do this, will you? Besides, you've been with the *rurales*, then the Apaches. I know how them white folks—Texans, especially— will take that. But if you've got money, it won't matter. Gold has a way of making things right."

"Indeed, it does," Fargo joined in, nodding at the girl.

"It's done, then," Sampson said. He lifted the jug and quickly filled all three cups. As they raised the mescal to their lips, he said, "Here's to Wells Fargo." Then he grinned at Fargo. "And to the One Who Moves Mountains. Let's hope he stays lucky—and out of poisoned water holes."

As Fargo threw the fiery liquid down his throat, he found himself looking at Carrie. She was watching him as well, her violet eyes glowing warmly. He had no difficulty understanding why

Sampson would be willing to take this chance for such a girl.

He reckoned that if he were in the old prospector's shoes, he would probably do the same damn thing.

7

Skip Turpin almost dropped the broom he was
using to sweep out the Wells Fargo office. Fargo
paused in the doorway and shucked his hat back
off his forehead as he grinned at the towheaded
clerk.

"Is Bridger around?"

"No, he ain't, Mr. Fargo. Hey, is that really
you?"

"It's me, all right," Fargo assured him. "You tell
Bridger I'll be in Miner's Haven."

"I sure will, Mr. Fargo."

As Fargo left the express office and started down
the street to the saloon, he heard Skip spreading
the news. Fargo had already left the pony he had
ridden in on at the livery stable, then gone to check
on his Ovaro. The pinto was in fine shape, he had
been pleased to note. Now, as he walked toward
the Miner's Haven, he could see the effect on oth-

ers as the news spread that he was back. When he reached the saloon finally, he found he had to push through an eager, watchful crowd on the porch before he could reach the batwings.

Shouldering through them, he paused a moment to let his eyes adjust to the dimness. Excited townsfolk pushed eagerly into the saloon behind him. Striding over to the bar, Fargo ordered a whiskey.

As the bottle was slapped down onto the bar in front of him, the barkeep peered curiously at him. "Ain't you that feller, Fargo? The one that rode shotgun for that gold shipment?"

Fargo pulled the bottle to him and filled his shot glass. Then he downed the whiskey. It helped some, but the alkali dust was still an inch thick all the way past his gullet. He poured himself another whiskey and poured this one down with the same dispatch.

"That's me," he said finally, fixing the barkeep with his cold blue eyes. "And right now I'm looking for Tim Bridger."

"He ain't here."

Behind him, Fargo heard a chair scrape suddenly. "Hey, mister!"

Turning, Fargo found himself looking into the wide-eyed face of the shotgun messenger whose place he had taken three weeks before, Rex Barry.

"You're him," Barry cried. "You're Skye Fargo. You took my place on that stage. Mister, I owe you a drink."

"Pleased to see you're up and about," Fargo said as Barry left his table and joined Fargo at the bar.

Everyone in the place was talking now, some

standing, others moving toward the bar, faces eager. More townsmen crowded in through the batwings.

Barry looked quickly around, a wide grin on his face. "The drinks are on me," he cried.

That broke the tension as the patrons in the saloon and those streaming in from outside crowded the bar. It took a while for Barry and Fargo to extricate themselves from the swarming prospectors and townspeople, each one of whom, it seemed, simply had to slap Fargo on the back or shake his hand.

At last, the two men were able to find a quiet table in a corner. Fargo waved over one of the bar girls and ordered a bottle. When she brought it, Fargo started to pay, but Barry would not allow it.

"Hey, now listen, Fargo. You can't pay for a drink in this town. I won't let you."

Fargo shrugged, and as Barry poured, Fargo looked more closely at the older man. There was a large welt over his right ear and a recently healed gash just over the temple. The hair about the gash had been shaven off and was now only a short stubble. Barry was lucky to be alive, Fargo realized, and he felt a sudden warmth for this old man who now wanted nothing better than to pay for his drinks.

"Welcome back to Gold City, Mr. Fargo."

Fargo turned to see Slade Kingston approaching his table, a cheroot in his mouth, a malevolent gleam in his lidded, calculating eyes. When he saw the look on Fargo's face, he smiled brightly, ingratiatingly, and came to a halt.

"No need to get riled, friend," Kingston said. "I harbor no ill will, I promise you. In a moment of weakness a few weeks ago, I turned with violence on a fellow human creature. I deeply regret my actions of that day."

He looked carefully around after that little speech and rocked back on his heels. He was obviously enjoying himself.

Fargo said nothing, perfectly willing to let the foolish son of a bitch dig his own grave.

"So, as I say," the gambler resumed, "let bygones be bygones. And so I say once again, welcome back, Mr. Fargo. You are, it appears, a most fortunate man. Even more remarkable—you are a sole survivor."

At that moment Sheriff Sands entered the saloon and pushed through the crowd to face Fargo.

"That's right, Fargo," the sheriff said bluntly. "Kingston's got a point. You're the only one left alive after that raise. The whiskey drummer and Bill Gifford are dead. The Apaches left them to the vultures. But you look just fine. You walk in here without a scratch."

"It wasn't Apaches attacked that stage."

"Oh?"

"It was Mullin and his gang."

"That so?"

"In that case, how come Mullin let you go?"

"This is no place to discuss that, Sheriff. I came in here looking for the express agent. Where's Bridger?"

"He'll be here soon enough. But I sure wish

you'd talk to me now. You're gonna have to do it sooner or later."

"What's the matter, Fargo?" asked Kingston. "Why can't you tell the sheriff here what happened?"

Fargo looked Kingston over, as if measuring him for a coffin. His patience had worn pretty thin by this time. The gambler saw the glint in Fargo's eyes and took a quick step back.

"No need to take offense, friend," he protested, smiling. "I'm just sorry you see fit to evade honest inquiry. All of us here would very much like to know how you were able to escape Mullin's gang."

"Yeah!" someone in back bellowed angrily. "How do you explain that, Fargo?"

Fargo looked away from the gambler and poured himself another drink.

"Hey!" someone yelled. "I saw him ride into the livery. That's an Apache war pony he rode in on."

Fargo threw the whiskey angrily down his throat, then poured himself another glass.

"That true, Fargo?" the sheriff demanded. "You ain't denyin' you rode in here on an Apache pony?"

"Why should I deny it?"

Someone else in the crowd spoke up. "You hear that? He admits it. He's in league with them murderin' savages."

"No wonder he's the only one came back," someone else shouted.

"Them Apaches killed my partner," an old-timer in back declared. "Some of you men here saw how he died and what was left by the time them heathen devils finished with him."

Others shouted out similar atrocities. It was not a pleasant litany. As each man recounted his own or a neighbor's torture, the faces of those surrounding Fargo darkened. After all, this man Fargo was the same man who—not too long before in this very same saloon—had called them all cowards, and worse.

Now it was their turn to wax indignant.

"Come on, you fellers," cried Rex Barry, looking pleadingly around at the ring of faces. "Leave us alone to finish this here bottle, why don't you? Go on, get out of here."

The crowd, a sullen, angry collection of frustrated gold miners by this time, had no quarrel with Rex Barry. Slowly, grudgingly, the men backed off. Kingston, making no effort to hide the pleased grin on his face, went back to his poker game. The sheriff left the saloon.

Fargo promptly poured Rex Barry a drink.

"Maybe that wasn't such a good idea, Rex," Fargo told him. "Sticking your neck out like that."

"You stuck it out for me."

Fargo nodded, then looked around at those sullen patrons that still remained in the saloon. "It sure don't take long to get this crowd riled, does it?"

"Not when the talk's about Apaches."

An occasional muttered comment carried across the room to them, but Fargo paid them no heed. He knew it wouldn't do to let himself get all riled. Not yet, anyway. He understood what these men were feeling. For them, the Apache were scarcely human—and they were unable to tolerate any man who could speak well of them. The worst thing one miner could call another was "Apache lover."

At that moment Bridger hurried into the saloon, caught sight of Fargo and Barry, and hurried over to their table, his hand extended.

"I just heard you got back," he said, shaking Fargo's hand. "May I join you?"

"Not here," said Fargo. "I think we'd better use your office."

"Of course. Follow me."

As Fargo got up, he thanked Rex for the drink. Rex was sorry to see him go, but there was something else in his eyes: a warning glint that alerted Fargo.

As Fargo settled in the chair by Bridger's desk, he found himself looking more closely at the ex-preacher and thinking of the warning in Rex Barry's eyes. Bridger was the man, after all, who had lied to him—and to Bill Gifford—when he let Fargo think there was no gold on that stage when he must have spent that entire night overseeing the gold's placement under the stagecoach's floorboards. Bridger had even gone to the length of selecting a brand-new coach so no one would wonder at all that hammering and activity in the dead of night.

Now, sitting before Fargo, Bridger presented his usual somber cast, his deep-set, brooding eyes regarding Fargo coldly. Fargo had little difficulty imagining the fire and brimstone this ex-preacher must have heaped upon his congregation every Sunday. As he unloaded on them, they undoubtedly felt the hell-fire blistering their feet.

"Well, now, Mr. Fargo," Bridger said, "judging from the temper of that crowd I met coming out of the saloon, you must have quite a story to tell. I'll want the full particulars, of course, to wire the company's headquarters in San Francisco."

Fargo told Bridger everything that had happened since he rode out of Gold City, not forgetting to mention Sampson Riley's offer to lead them to Diablo Canyon for a percentage of the recovered gold. When Fargo finished, he saw a frown darken Bridger's face.

"I don't know if San Francisco will go for a percentage of the gold," he said. "After all, that gold does not belong to Wells Fargo. But I am certain they will be most generous if that old coot can lead us to it."

"I think Sampson will want your assurance—and gold on delivery."

"Mmm. Well, I'll just have to see what I can do. You understand my position, of course. I am just one small agent in a very large empire. But if what you say is true—the Mullin gang has been wiped out—and if the Apaches are willing to allow our coaches to go through their country unmolested—"

"That's what Sampson thinks. It was Mullin's gang who burned down that way station. They just wanted to make it look like the Apaches done it."

"Yes, and I believe you." He pursed his lips and regarded Fargo with some favor. "This is certainly excellent news, Mr. Fargo. Recovery of the gold would be quite a feather in all our caps. Wells Fargo would certainly appreciate all that you and this Sampson fellow have done in that regard."

"We'll need a few men to go with us."

"Of course. And mules. I'll see who I can round up. The sheriff will be willing to help in that, I'm sure."

"I suggest we leave first thing in the morning," Fargo told him. "We have to hurry, you realize. Naratena's gone now, but there's no telling when he'll be back."

Bridger nodded and got to his feet. "I agree. Are you staying at the hotel?"

Fargo got up also. "Yes. And the first thing I want to do now is visit the barbershop and get myself a hot bath."

"I can imagine." The dour agent managed a feeble smile. "All right, then. I'll be in touch."

Fargo clapped his hat back on and left the express office. His body was already itching to feel the delicious warmth of that hot, sudsy water rolling down his back and over his face. It had been a long, long time since he'd had a real steaming bath, and he was looking forward to it.

At first Fargo thought the barber had simply made a mistake—an honest miscalculation. But when he poured the second bucket of scalding hot water into the tub, Fargo knew that the barber was deliberately trying to boil him alive.

As the man reared back and waited for Fargo's reaction, Fargo smiled at him and said, "Let's have the next bucketful a little hotter."

The barber was an enormously stout fellow with a large, fleshy, clean-shaven face, the cheeks hanging on his side in great dewlaps, and three vast chins. Except for two crescents of white hair above each ear, he was shiny bald. He looked down at Fargo through eyes that looked like holes poked in snow.

"You want more?" he asked, a faint sneer on his face.

"You heard me."

"Why, sure, Mr. Fargo. Just you sit there a minute."

Wheezing, the barber turned and waddled back for more water. By the time he returned, Fargo was well lathered. The barber was holding the bucket with both hands and was lugging it with great care, making sure not to splash any of it on his apron. The steam from it moistened his pasty face.

As the barber neared the tub, Fargo rose up, and with one quick movement reached out with his left hand and grabbed the bucket from the barber. With his right hand, he caught the barber around the back of his neck, clutching securely onto one of the several ropes of fat encircling it. Forcing the barber's head down into the tub, Fargo dumped the near-boiling contents of the bucket over the barber's bald dome. The barber managed to pull his head up momentarily, blowing and squealing in sheer panic, but Fargo threw aside the empty bucket and, using both hands now, forced the barber's head back under the now truly scalding water.

The barber struggled violently, desperately, until

his thrashing bulk managed to pull the steel tub over onto its side. As the water spilled out, Fargo released the man and stepped back. The barber, squealing like a piglet on the run, staggered to his feet. Fargo threw him a towel. The man snatched it and wiped furiously at his pendulous face.

"You," he panted wildly. "You almost drowned me. That water is scalding."

Fargo grinned. "I was just trying to boil some of that tallow off you, mister."

"You were what?"

"You heard me. Now, I'd be much obliged if you'd set that tub back up and bring me some more water. Only this time I want the right temperature."

The barber's cries had drawn a crowd from the barbershop. They could see through the open doorway of the back shed. Two burly miners entered and stood in the doorway, lather still on their faces, arms folded. It was clear how they regarded Fargo—with barely suppressed anger. Righteous anger.

"You all right, Bert?" one of the two men inquired.

"No, I ain't, Ray," the barber replied angrily. "This here Apache-lovin' son of a bitch tried to drown me in this tub. Said the water was too hot."

"That so?" Ray said, looking at Fargo with predatory eyes. "Maybe we ought to cook him a little—turn him into a real redskin."

"Yeah," said his partner, flashing his yellow buck teeth.

The two men took a step into the rear shed and started toward Fargo. Fargo loosened his shoulders, making ready. But before the fun could begin, the sheriff hustled into the bath shed.

"What's goin' on here?" he demanded of the barber.

"This here Fargo assaulted me, Sheriff," Bert told him.

"That so?" the sheriff asked, turning on Fargo, his dark eyes gleaming belligerently from under his beetling brows.

Fargo shrugged. "The son of a bitch tried to scald me."

"Hell, that ain't nothin'. Bert's just trying to please. We're always after him for not heatin' the water enough. Maybe with you, he was just trying to make sure you didn't have no complaint."

"That ain't it, Sheriff, and you know it."

The sheriff looked back at Bert. "Well, Bert, it's up to you. Do you want to press charges?"

"I sure do. That man should be locked up."

The sheriff looked back at Fargo. He smiled bleakly. "You heard Bert. I ain't got no choice."

"What's the charge?"

"Disturbing the peace. Assault and battery."

"If you need any help with this son of a bitch, Charlie," Ray said, wiping the lather from his face, "Harry and I'll be glad to lend a hand."

"Never mind that," the sheriff told them. "Just keep out of this. I can handle Fargo." Then he looked back at Fargo. "You'd best get dressed and come with me. For your own good. It don't look like you're any too popular around here."

A moment later the sheriff marched Fargo, fully dressed, ahead of him back through the barbershop and onto the sidewalk. A large crowd had gathered by this time—every man in it eager to see the sheriff march Fargo off to the jailhouse. From the rear of the crowd an apple core sailed, catching Fargo just under his left cheekbone. Then a rock followed, narrowly missing Fargo's head. He did not flinch, just kept on walking.

The sheriff, just behind Fargo, nudged him out into the street. "Better hurry it up," he warned. "If the men in this crowd get a hold of you, they'll rip you apart and dance on the pieces. And there won't be a damn thing I can do about it."

Fargo reached the boardwalk on the other side of the street and started along it to the jail. Ahead of him a bulge in the crowd lapped the boardwalk. A red-faced whiskey-sodden prospector stepped out of the crowd and into Fargo's path. Fargo kept going. When the man wouldn't move aside, Fargo pushed him out of his way.

The miner swore and took a wild swing at him. Fargo ducked easily, then slashed the blade of his right hand down on the side of the old miner's neck in a quick, vicious rabbit punch. As the man sagged, Fargo picked him up, raised him over his head, and hurled him at the crowd closing in on him. The body struck three men in the front ranks. They staggered back under the weight of their flailing burden, then sagged to the ground.

The crowd had been simmering until that moment. Now it began to boil. As it surged forward, the sheriff pushed Fargo quickly toward the jailhouse. A few managed to grab hold of him, but Fargo shook them off and kept going. By the time he reached the jailhouse and was hustled through the door, the mob was calling out to the sheriff, demanding Fargo be given over to them. Glancing back, Fargo saw the whiskey-primed blood lust on every face.

Nothing less than a lynching would satisfy them now.

8

Sheriff Sands slammed the office door shut on the mob outside, then deftly lifted Fargo's six-gun from his holster. Fargo spun around to find himself staring into the unblinking muzzle of Sheriff Sands' six-gun.

"Put down that gun, Sheriff," Fargo told him sharply. "There's no need for that."

Sands tossed Fargo's revolver onto his desk.

"That ain't the way I see it," Sands replied, a hard, unrelenting gleam in his small dark eyes.

It was not easy for Fargo to keep his temper, but he managed. "Now, you know what happened, Sheriff. There's no mystery to it. The barber tried to boil me, and now we've got a crowd out there yellin' for my scalp. The way I see it, your job is not to lock me up, but just keep the peace."

"Maybe, but that ain't the only reason I brought you in here, Fargo."

"What's the other reason?"

"I'm curious. You still ain't explained to my satisfaction what happened out there with them Apaches. All I know for sure is two men are dead, the gold is missing, and you turn up as bright as a new penny, trying to drown Bert in his own bathtub."

"Go see Tim Bridger. I told him what happened. And I don't feel like going over it again. Fact is, he'll be looking you up soon enough."

Sands studied Fargo's face for a long moment, then waggled his gun at him. "All right, then. Turn around and march into the cell block. Take the first cell."

"Damn it, Sands, you know that ain't necessary."

"Maybe so, but right now, your word ain't worth much around here . . . or hadn't you noticed."

Fargo entered the cell block and walked into the first cell. As soon as he was locked securely behind bars, the sheriff smiled in at him. "Just look at it this way, Fargo. Now you'll be able to keep out of trouble—at least for a while."

The sheriff left the cell block, and a moment later Fargo heard him step to the door of his office and pull it open. The noise of the crowd, which had kept to a fairly steady level until then, swelled to a crescendo as the sheriff appeared in the doorway.

Fargo heard the sheriff shouting something to the crowd. It sounded like he was warning them. A ragged dialogue followed and Fargo was able to catch only a few words. Finally the door closed behind the sheriff as the man moved off through the crowd.

About ten minutes later, the door opened. Above the crowd's mutter, Fargo heard the tramp of heavy boots as at least two men hurried into the small building. A moment later Rex and Skip Turpin entered the cell block. They were carrying shotguns.

"Sands asked for two deputies to help out," Rex told Fargo. "So Skip and I volunteered. That's sure a mean crowd out there."

"First things first," Fargo told them. "Get me out of this cell."

Skip cleared his throat nervously. "I don't know if the sheriff wants us to do that," he said.

Ignoring Skip, Rex turned and left the cell block. He returned with a key and unlocked the cell door. Fargo hurried into the sheriff's office, grabbed his Colt, and dropped it into his holster.

He turned to Rex. "I got a bad feeling about the sheriff. I don't think he's coming back. If things get any more heated up out there, I'm making a break for it."

"I don't blame you."

"I'll need my horse and the rest of my gear."

"Where's your horse?"

"In the Wells Fargo horse barn. The Sharps and the rest of my gear is upstairs in my hotel room."

Rex understood at once. "I got you," he said. "Give me time to slip out and fetch your gear from the hotel. Then I can saddle up your horse."

Fargo nodded and handed Rex the key to his room. "Best thing to do is wait for me in the barn. If I make a break for it, that's where I'll be headed."

Rex nodded. "Fargo, there's something I been

meanin' to tell you. I was going to do it in the saloon, but you lit out with Bridger before I could get a word out."

A stone crashed through the window.

"Jesus!" cried Skip.

"Tell me later, Rex," Fargo told the old man. "We don't have much time, it looks like. Right now, I need a horse and the rest of my gear, that Sharps, especially."

Rex nodded quickly and turned to Skip. "You think you can hold the fort, Skip?" he asked.

"Sure," Skip insisted stoutly. "Don't you worry about me."

Rex clapped the young man on the back, then flipped his shotgun to Fargo and hurried out of the building. Fargo moved cautiously to the window and watched as Rex pushed his way through the crowd on his way down the street.

Moving up beside Fargo, Skip peered out also. "There's sure a lot of angry people out there."

Fargo nodded and stepped back from the window. "There'll be a lot more before long."

It was getting pretty dark now and someone had started to harangue the crowd. Fargo recognized the voice. It was Slade Kingston's. Cheers of affirmation punctuated the gambler's words; and from the sound of it, Kingston was doing one hell of a job of whipping the mob into a frenzy—not that it had really needed all that much encouragement.

Fargo strode to the window and peered out. He could see Kingston across the street. Two men were standing beside him, holding torches. Fargo watched Kingston for a moment, then spoke to Skip over his shoulder.

"I don't like the look of it, Skip. If I were you, I'd get the hell out of here. Now."

Skip hurried to the window and peered out himself. By this time the crowd's roar was almost constant. Other, more strident voices were out-shouting Kingston by this time. Abruptly, the crowd turned and a sea of torchlit heads and shoul-ders surged across the street toward the jailhouse. A second rock broke through the window, this one thrown so hard it slammed into the far wall. Another rock thudded against the door.

Skip's eyes grew wide. Fargo could see he was close to panic, but he was game, all the same. "I'm not runnin' out on you now, Mr. Fargo," he insisted.

"I appreciate that, Skip." He checked the shot-gun's load one more time and flicked off the safety.

"Open the door," he told Skip. "Then stand aside and keep your head down."

"But, Mr. Fargo, they'll—"

"Do as I say."

Unhappily, Skip threw back the bolt, unlatched the door, then pulled it open. As he stepped to one side, Fargo strode past him and paused in the open doorway. Startled at the sight of Fargo standing before them fully armed, the crowd scrambled to a halt. The torches cast a livid glow over those men standing just in front of the porch. With silent con-tempt, Fargo hefted his shotgun and surveyed the crowd.

Their eyes bright with fear, those closest took a

hasty step backward as they saw Fargo's finger coiled about both triggers on his shotgun. Fargo looked out over the crowd, searching for Slade Kingston. But the gambler was gone, his work here finished.

Or so he must have thought.

Fargo looked back down into the faces of those men nearest him. In town after town, it seemed, he had come upon these same grizzled, whiskey-sodden faces. The only things really clean about them were the gleaming six-guns strapped to their thighs.

But what marked them for certain were their eyes.

In them Fargo found no humor, no joy, no honor, no courage—only cynicism and suspicion. They were the eyes of men already dead, for most of these men believed in nothing. Instead of courage they were filled with empty bluster. The only talent they possessed was a mean ability to prey on weaker men, and whenever they moved against one another or their betters, they did so from ambush.

"All right, gents," Fargo told them mildly, "why don't you just turn around and go about your business?"

"Why should we?" someone in back demanded.

Another bravo shouted, "We're gonna string you up, Fargo."

Fargo shrugged almost negligently and brought up his shotgun, allowing its twin bores to sweep slowly over the crowd.

"I got here nine buck to the barrel," Fargo

informed them almost gently. "The first one takes another step closer ain't liable to see the next sun come up."

A skinny old-timer shouted, "You can't kill us all."

"Maybe not," Fargo replied, "but the spread will make enough of you dead to satisfy me."

That statement, uttered quietly and without bravado, struck a chill into the crowd. Every man looking up at Fargo's solid figure knew that if push came to shove, Fargo would not hesitate to use his weapon. Hell, what did he have to lose? As this obvious fact sank in, the crowd lost its enthusiasm.

One miner turned abruptly and pushed his way back through the crowd, heading toward one of the saloons down the street. "The hell with this," he said, "I'm thirsty."

With that, the tension broke and the entire crowd began to pull back.

One man, however, remained standing where he was, his feet planted wide apart. Squat, somewhat bowlegged, he was sporting a bushy black beard, and his eyes were as hard as steel, his face flushed with alcohol.

For some reason, nailing Fargo obviously meant a lot more to him than it did to any of the others—and it wasn't just the liquor. It occurred to Fargo that he was probably one of those who had lost a friend or a loved one to the Apache and had decided to his satisfaction that nailing Fargo was one way for him to settle that score.

The dispersing crowd suddenly congealed as every man swung around to watch the black-bearded man standing entirely alone in the middle of the street, less than ten yards from Fargo. Those behind him scattered quickly to get out of the line of fire.

"I hate Apaches," the man told Fargo, his voice grating harshly. "And I don't tolerate them that sides with 'em. No Apache-lover is goin' to send me away with my tail between my legs."

"Easy, feller," Fargo said. "Think a minute."

"Why should I?"

"I've got the drop on you."

"Hell, you have," the man cried.

His hand flashed across his body. Drunk or not, he was fast. But though his six-gun was free of leather in an instant, it was still coming up when both barrels of Fargo's shotgun spat flame and smoke. The bearded fellow's shirtfront went suddenly dark. The buckshot almost cut him in two. As he was flung back, he sagged pitifully, then toppled to the ground.

A roar of fury swept through the crowd. For a moment the men wavered, seemingly undecided as to what they should do. Then someone shouted to them in anger, reminding them that Fargo's shotgun was now empty. At once, they surged back across the street toward the jailhouse.

Fargo flung down the empty shotgun and, drawing his Colt, darted off the porch and cut down the alley alongside the jailhouse. Someone stepped out of the shadows with his six-gun raised. Fargo slugged him to the ground with one swipe of his gun barrel and ducked into the alley, heading for the Wells Fargo stables.

The crowd surged after him. Shots were fired. Splinters exploded from the side of an outhouse as he raced past it. Just ahead of him in the shadow of a doorway, he caught the dull gleam of a gun barrel. He fired at it and heard a groan and the sound of a six-gun clattering to the ground.

Two horses appeared, galloping down the alley toward him. Cheers came from behind Fargo as the crowd assumed Fargo was now trapped. The horses loomed closer and Fargo saw it was Rex on a big chestnut, leading Fargo's Ovaro.

Reaching Fargo, Rex pulled up, then wheeled his horse in the narrow alley and tossed the pinto's reins to Fargo. Mounting on the run, Fargo clapped his heels to the pinto and took after Rex. From behind them in the alley came cries of outrage and disappointment, followed by a sudden, angry fusillade. A moment later they raced out of the alley and turned up Main Street.

A knot of four or five men were standing irresolutely in front of the Miner's Haven. Fargo promptly headed right for them. The men rushed for cover. As Fargo and Rex galloped past the Miner's Haven, a quick flurry of gunfire exploded from it. One round struck a street lamp beside Fargo, shattering it. Fargo looked back. A few men were racing after them down the middle of the street, but so far, there was no sign of an organized pursuit.

But Fargo was not taking any chances. Urging his pinto to go still faster, he raced full out through the night.

They were topping a rise about two miles from

Gold City when Fargo realized that Rex was having trouble keeping up. Fargo reined in and galloped back to meet him.

"What's wrong, Rex?"

"I was hit back there."

Fargo slid quickly to the ground and reached up to help Rex down. The man's dead weight almost toppled Fargo as he guided Rex to a sitting position under a scrub pine, then propped his back up against it. Fargo went back to his horse for his canteen. Unscrewing the cap, he lifted the canteen to Rex's lips.

"Thanks," Rex managed, gulping gratefully at the water.

"Where were you hit?"

"The slug hit me in the back and rode up into my lung, feels like," Rex told him. "But never mind that. I got somethin' to tell you."

"Can't it wait? You sound pretty rough."

"No, it can't. I already waited too long. I been sniffin' around, Fargo, and I think I know what's been goin' on around here—about that Mullin gang, I mean."

"I'm listening."

"I think Bridger was workin' with the Mullin gang. That's how Mullin knew the gold was on that stage. I figure Bridger was tippin' Mullin off about each gold shipment. That's why that Pinkerton was snoopin' around."

"The Pinkerton?"

"The whiskey drummer. Only he wasn't no drummer. He told me he was hired by the Wells

Fargo office in San Francisco to check on all the holdups."

Fargo suddenly found himself recalling the sheriff boosting the barely conscious drummer up into the stagecoach. If the sheriff was in this with Bridger, he would have known that before long the Mullin gang would be taking care of the Pinkerton.

Rex went on. "And that trouble you had with the barber just now. It was a setup to get rid of you. All the saloons in town are bein' paid good to prime that mob with free booze."

"Where's Bridger now?"

"I heard he rode out of town."

At once Fargo knew where Bridger and the sheriff were—or, better yet, where they were headed.

"What about Kingston?" Fargo asked. "You think he's in this with Bridger?"

Rex began to cough. A thin trickle of blood began to trail out of one corner of his mouth. "Wouldn't surprise me none," he managed.

"Was this what you wanted to tell me in the sheriff's office?"

Rex nodded feebly. All of a sudden he could not seem to stop coughing. And soon he was doubling over with each paroxysm. He sounded as if his lungs were being ripped into pieces with each cough. Fargo tried to give Rex more water, but Rex pushed the canteen away and glanced miserably up at Fargo.

"Go on without me, Fargo," he rasped painfully.

"No."

"Go on, I'm tellin' you," he insisted. "There ain't nothing you can do for me."

"Dammit, I can't leave you like this, Rex."

"Hell! I'm gonna die! Ain't no sense in denyin' it, and if its all the same to you, I'd prefer doin' it alone."

"It just don't seem right."

"I told you," Rex gasped. "They ain't nothin' you can do. You'd let a dog crawl away and die in peace. Why can't you give me the same consideration?"

Fargo stood up and looked down at Rex. Though he understood, that didn't make it any easier for him. He had saved this old man once, and now, in repaying him, Rex had given his life. There were things Fargo wanted to say, but he could not find the right words. A desolation fell over him.

"If that's what you want, Rex."

Rex began to cough again. He looked up and managed a weak nod, then waved Fargo off.

Reluctantly, Fargo returned to their horses. Looking back, he saw the old man roll away from the tree and lay his head down on the hard ground. The ragged, tearing sound of his coughing cut through the night.

Fargo unsaddled Rex's chestnut and transferred the man's canteen and leather water bag to his pinto. Then he slapped the chestnut on the rump to send it back to town, mounted his Ovaro, and rode off. When he looked back for the last time, Rex's figure had been swallowed up by the darkness.

As he urged his pinto on through the night, he knew that all he could hope for now was that he might reach Sampson's cabin before Bridger and the sheriff did. As Fargo had been foolish enough

113

to reveal to the Wells Fargo agent, they would need Sampson to show them the way to Diablo Canyon. And it wasn't likely that either man would allow Sampson the luxury of refusing, not with all that gold at stake.

Sampson's mistrust of Bridger, it seemed, had been well-founded.

9

Bridger was well inside the Devil's playground. Astride a powerful bay, he was leading four pack mules.

He was betraying Wells Fargo, the sheriff, and Kingston, but such considerations no longer mattered. This would be only one more step further down the path of damnation he had been following the moment he conspired with Bart Mullin's gang. By now Bridger had become a fatalist. He regarded himself as already doomed, his soul corrupted beyond all redemption.

Seven years before, Bridger had come West as a married minister of the Calvinist persuasion. In his arrogance and pride he had sought out the rowdiest, most godforsaken sink of iniquity in which to begin his ministry: Devil's Gap, a booming mining town of four thousand souls deep in the Nevada mountains. The inhabitants were hurtling toward perdition with a willing, happy abandon, ably aided and abetted in this endeavor by twelve brothels, over ten gambling dens, and close to nineteen saloons.

As he had complained to his wife, he would never know when Sunday came if he didn't keep track of the days religiously. His church was an abandoned feed mill on the outskirts of town and so empty of parishioners that in desperation he attempted to bring his ministry to the afflicted souls who dwelt in the town's infamous brothels and gaming houses.

His efforts brought only hoots of derision at first, and when he persisted, much worse. He had pots of night soil emptied on his head. Whiskey was forcibly poured down his protesting throat. More than once he had ridden home without his trousers. Yet nothing could discourage him, it seemed. He returned to his task each day with renewed determination, never questioning the attraction the saloons and brothels held for him. So innocent was he, after all, of the workings of that dark master of them all, Satan.

At last he tasted success—or what he thought was success—when the most infamous and wealthy madam in the town of Devil's Gap confessed to him her wish to follow Jesus. Bridger ministered to her for a full week. He prayed with her, ate with her, kept himself on hand to be at her side whenever she weakened, listening all the while with mounting horror to the lurid accounts of her incredible licentiousness, which poured in a steady stream from her tormented soul.

On the sixth night, while he slept fitfully, she had come to his bed, craving a boon—a small favor, as she put it. The weakness of her flesh was threatening to overwhelm her. Perhaps he could see it in his heart to minister with as much devotion to her body as he had to her soul.

He had never returned to the feed mill—or to his wife.

And only gradually was he able to pull himself out of the awful degradation he found in that harlot's arms and construct another mask to cover the ravaged wasteland that was now his soul. His education came to his aid at this juncture, and he found employment first as a newspaperman and then as an agent with the Wells Fargo Company.

But the devil had him in his palm now, and there was no sense in denying his awesome power. There was not the slightest doubt in Bridger's mind that he was damned for all eternity. Therefore, he was determined to make the best use possible of what time still remained to him on this accursed planet.

The moon climbed into the sky, its great baleful cat's eye burning down on him, sending its silver sheen ahead of him along the road. It was Satan's eye, of course, sending this aid to one of his own. Abruptly, the moon vanished behind one of the two buttes that flanked the road ahead. As he rode into the inky blackness between the two towering rock masses, a voice called to him softly from the darkness to his right.

"Howdy, Bridger," said the sheriff.

Pulling up hastily, Bridger peered into the blackness. "My God! Is that you, Sands?"

The sheriff, astride his big black, rode out of the shadows, a wintry smile on his face. "I see you got the mules easy enough." His face hardened. "But I thought you told me it was going to take you until tomorrow morning to get them."

"It . . . didn't take as long as I thought it would, so I decided I'd better not waste any time."

The sheriff chuckled meanly. "Don't bullshit me, Bridger."

"Dammit, Sands, you'd a done the same thing if you were me. Where's Kingston?"

"He'll be along. I left him behind to whip up that crowd some more. It won't take much." Sands glanced up at the moon and grinned. "That's sure as hell a lyncher's moon up there."

"You're sure that mob will lynch Fargo?"

"No, I'm not. They'll more than likely roast him first. I never saw a town more whipped up."

"So let's get moving."

"No. We're waiting for Kingston."

Bridger took a deep breath and did his best to bottle his anger—and his disappointment. To share this gold with Sands and Kingston had not been his intention at all.

He dismounted wearily and led his horse and the pack mules into the shadows, then slumped down upon the ground, his back against the rock. The sheriff followed in after him, dismounted, and hunkered down beside him. The two men no longer had anything to say to each other.

Both men heard the sound of a lone rider's hoofbeats at the same time. Sands unholstered his Colt and got quickly to his feet, then flattened himself back against the wall. As the rider got closer, he cocked the revolver. Approaching the twin rock formation, the rider slowed to a canter, then to a walk. The dark figure appeared on the trail, outlined sharply against the moonlit rocks behind him.

"Sands!" Kingston called out as he pulled up. "You in there?"

Uncocking and holstering his revolver, Sands said, "We're in here. Stay on your horse."

Bridger and Sands mounted up and rode out of the shadows to meet Kingston. Kingston grinned when he saw Bridger and the mules trailing behind him.

"I see you guessed right, Sands," Kingston told the sheriff.

"Wasn't difficult. How'd it go at the jail?"

"Nothing to worry about. When I pulled out, the crowd was moving to the jailhouse. I think they just might tear that Apache-lover apart before they manage to fit a noose around his neck."

Satisfied, the sheriff turned to Bridger. "Just how far is it to Sampson Riley's place?"

"We should reach it before dawn."

"Then let's go."

The badlands were just ahead of Fargo—a red tangle of peaks and buttes gleaming in the first light of morning. His Ovaro had settled into a punishing downhill lope as the trail dropped into another steep canyon, and Fargo was anxious to keep going. But the sight of water south of the trail, rushing white across a rocky ford, caused him to leave the trail and ride toward it.

A few feet back from the stream, he dismounted. Keeping his horse well back from the water, he dropped his bandanna into the stream, wrung it out, then soaked the pinto's muzzle with it. Only then did Fargo allow the horse to lower his muzzle into the water. After watching the animal carefully for a moment, he pulled him back. Then he tied him up away from the stream. And then he slaked his own thirst in the icy, teeth-chilling water and filled both canteens and the water bag.

He was pleased he had found this running water. He preferred it to a water holes seasoned with Naratena's poison. Mounting up, he allowed the pinto to drink its fill, then pushed on.

He soon found himself high in the badlands. The game trail he was following flowed around outcroppings of rock and across a crimson plateau slashed by winding, sheer-walled draws, deceptive and deadly as pitfalls. The trail kept him moving steadily on past the breaks, finding always the natural, safest way around, and through the tangle of boulders and canyons. It was the same route Sampson had suggested he take on his ride back to Gold City. Fargo expected to see Sampson's adobe cabin ahead of him before long.

He crested a low butte and saw the cabin below him. One glance and he pulled up swiftly and dismounted. There were five horses and four mules clustered about the cabin's entrance. Fargo hurried back off the skyline with his pinto, tied it to a sapling, then returned to the rim of the butte and peered over.

He was just in time to see Carrie and Sampson, followed by Bridger, Sands, and Kingston, leave the cabin. With the three men watching, Carrie and Sampson mounted up first. Then the sheriff set about tying both Sampson's and Carrie's hands to their saddle horns. Only then did the three men mount up. With Sampson in the lead, they moved off across the flat, the mules following behind.

There was no question where they were heading: to Diablo Canyon.

The Trailsman mounted up and, keeping below the rim of the butte, followed after them. After a few miles, he left the butte and found a ridge paralleling the course Sampson was following. Keeping off the skyline whenever possible, he trailed them for the rest of the morning, waiting for them to camp for the noon meal. But Bridger and his two companions were too eager to reach the gold. They pressed on through the heat of midday without pause.

Fargo began noticing landmarks that told him he was within a few miles of Diablo Canyon. At the same time he became aware of how much more slowly the caravan below him was moving across the heat-blasted flat. Fargo understood. It was the heat. It had been bothering him as well.

A mile farther on, the caravan came to a halt, then broke from the trail and headed toward a cluster of rocks just below it. Fargo swore softly. They were heading toward the same water hole Fargo had used earlier, the one Naratena had poisoned.

He didn't care about the others, but he couldn't let Carrie and Sampson drink from that water hole.

Despite the heat, the Trailsman urged the Ovaro to a canter and circled the rocks enclosing the water hole until he was approaching it with the sun at his back. Dismounting in a gully, he snaked his Sharps from its scabbard and hurried closer to the water hole. It was on the far side of a wide canyon floor. When he was within two hundred yards of the water hole, Fargo caught sight of the five approaching it through the rocks. Loading swiftly, he rested the gun on the top of a low boulder and sighted carefully at a spot just in front of the lead rider, Sampson.

Hang on, old-timer, Fargo thought as he squeezed the trigger.

The detonation was like a crack of thunder as its echo slammed off the rocks. The ground just in front of Sampson's horse exploded. The horse reared, but Sampson managed to stay in the saddle. Swiftly dropping in another cartridge, Fargo sent another slug at them, this one higher. Above the powerful blast of the Sharps, he heard the round ricochet off the rocks.

His next shot grazed one of their mules. It screamed like something human. Fargo did not like to do it, but he had to make it clear to Bridger and the sheriff that they had better retreat from the water hole, no matter how thirsty they were.

They got the message. Pulling their horses around, the five riders rode back up the slope to the trail. Fargo sent one more round after them, careful to make it close enough for them to hear its ricochet, but not so close as to endanger Carrie or Sampson. As they disappeared into the rocks, Fargo stood up and watched as a lone rider he took to be the sheriff peeled away from the rest of them and headed in Fargo's direction. In a moment he had lost himself in the rocks, but Fargo wasn't fooled. The sheriff was still coming after him.

Fine.

Fargo checked to make sure he had a sufficient supply of cartridges and set off on foot to intercept the sheriff. He moved swiftly back along the floor of the gully until he was able to dart into some cover and cross the canyon floor, using the sheer wall for cover. Scrambling up a steep slope, he kept going until he was certain he was above the trail he had seen the sheriff take. He found a perch on a precarious ledge, loaded the Sharps, and waited.

It was not long before he heard, then saw, the sheriff riding cautiously along the trail beneath him. The sheriff appeared quite nervous. Abruptly, the lawman dismounted, pulled his rifle out of his scabbard, and peered off the trail down into the rocks below him. Fargo waited, hoping the man would ride closer. He would like to take the sheriff with only one shot, if possible.

After a moment or two, the sheriff mounted up again, then continued toward Fargo. Fargo cocked the rifle, lifted it up to his cheek, then tucked the stock into his shoulder. He was sighting along the barrel when he felt the ledge shift dangerously beneath his weight, and he realized that if he fired, there was a chance he would dislodge the rock on which he crouched, sending it crashing down the slope.

Swiftly, he lowered the weapon and straightened up, intent on moving back off the ledge to the slope beside him. But he was too late. As soon as he stood up, the ledge grunted sullenly, slipped forward, held for a moment, then gave way entirely. Fargo flung his rifle back up the slope and grabbed for the root of a pine beside him. But he was too late as the ledge broke free and went tumbling down the slope.

Fargo struck hard on his right shoulder once, felt himself tumbling, and came to a halt abruptly as he slammed into a small clump of juniper three-quarters of the way down the slope. Clinging to the juniper, he watched the ledge smash its way to the trail below, then crunch through the brush and disappear below the trail.

Sheriff Sands was already off his mount, racing up the slope toward Fargo, his six-gun out. He fired up at Fargo. Fargo ducked low and drew his own Colt. Returning Sands' fire, he plunged down the rest of the slope toward him. Sands fired again. As the slug whined past his cheek, Fargo fired a second time. But his gun misfired. Without slowing down, he threw the useless hunk of metal at Sands, then dived headfirst down the slope at the sheriff.

Sands straightened to meet Fargo's hurtling bulk, but Fargo caught him waist high, bowling him backward. Sands dropped his gun as both men tumbled wildly down the slope until they struck the trail.

The two men scrambled to their feet and began lashing out at each other. Fargo's first caught Sands on the head, rocking him back a couple of steps. Then Sands rushed Fargo. Fargo stood his ground and started punching Sands in the body. It did little good. Though Sands was smaller than Fargo, he had the heft and stability of a sack of cement. Grunting, Sands pushed free of Fargo, cutting at him with two quick jabs. Fargo ducked, bore in, and caught Sands repeatedly about the head and shoulders. Sands reeled back. As he did so, Fargo caught him with a looping right, stunning him. As he sagged, Fargo brought up his knee, catching Sands in the face and snapping his head back. A sudden, steady flow of blood poured from one nostril. Gasping, Sands staggered back until he slammed into a rock face.

Fargo moved in to finish him. But Sands rolled to one side and brought his own knee up, catching Fargo in the groin. Fargo gasped and doubled up. Now it was Sands' turn. Pushing away from the boulder, he began pounding Fargo with murderous, pistonlike punches about the head and face. Not a little astonished at the lawman's resiliency, Fargo hunched his shoulders, put his head down, and bore in past the man's flailing punches, swiping at him with a dogged, deadly precision.

For a moment the two stood toe to toe, Fargo's powerful, pistonlike arms driving through Sands' guard with great slogging blows, each blow jarring Sands clear to the base of his spine. The man began to collapse. Doggedly, Sands pulled himself together and drove a smashing blow into Fargo's face. It raked Fargo's cheekbone, skidded past, and ripped his ear.

Ignoring it, Fargo stepped in still closer. A stubborn, killing anger had taken over now and he hardly felt Sands' punches as he continued to pound him. Driving Sands away from the rock, Fargo forced him to stand on his own feet as he absorbed Fargo's relentless pounding. By this time, the sheriff's face had become raw meat. Sands' nose was shattered and both eyes were peering out from behind purpling, rapidly swelling ridges.

But the sheriff was game.

Somehow, he caught sight of his revolver. It had dropped onto the trail and was almost within reach. With a desperate wrench, he ducked under Fargo's punches, knocked him to one side, then pounced on the gun. Whirling around, his hand wavering, he fired at Fargo. The shot went wild as Fargo lunged forward and grabbed the gun, twisting it out of Sands' grasp.

Then, with one vicious swipe of the gun barrel, Fargo caught the sheriff on the side of his head, slamming him to the ground.

Fargo cocked the weapon and pointed it down at what remained of Sands' face. But the sheriff made no effort to get up. Then Fargo saw the unnatural depression in the side of Sands' skull and the look in his eyes. They were staring, unblinking, up at Fargo. Lowering the six-gun, Fargo stepped back a few paces, his shoulders heaving, his breath coming in great, rasping gasps. Sands was now looking past him—far past him at the sky above and whatever lay beyond.

And he would be doing so forever.

As Bridger watched the sheriff ride off, he turned to Sampson and the others. "We'll wait a minute. Whoever that was will be so busy with the sheriff, he won't have a chance to keep us from that water hole."

"Wouldn't advise that, Bridger," Sampson drawled, shoving his sombrero off his forehead.

"Why not, old man?" snapped Kingston.

"I just figured who that was over there."

"Well?"

"He was usin' a Sharps. I can tell from the sound of one—and the accuracy."

"So?"

"Fargo told me he'd left his Sharps in Gold City. He told me just before he rode out when I offered him my rifle. That feller firing at us was Fargo."

"Impossible," snapped Kingston.

Sampson grinned. "Yep. Looks like that lynch

mob got cold feet. Don't pay to let someone else do your dirty work, Kingston. It don't usually get done."

"But why would Fargo fire on you and this girl here?" Bridger demanded.

"To stop us from drinkin' from that water hole. It's poisoned."

"How would he know that?"

"He drank from it himself and almost died. It was Naratena's Zuni medicine man what saved him. I didn't know which water hole it was he drank from, but I do now."

Bridger and Kingston looked nervously down the slope at the water hole, then back to Sampson.

"How far is it to water from here?" Bridger asked.

"There's water inside Diablo Canyon. Take us another couple of hours. And I suggest we get a move on if we want to reach it before nightfall."

"All right, then," Bridger said. " Let's move out."

"Aren't you going to wait for the sheriff?" Kingston asked Bridger.

"Sands can take care of himself," Bridger insisted. "I say we move out now. I want to get at that water. I'm dry as a bone."

With a shrug, Kingston looked at Sampson. "All right, old man. Show us the way."

They were some distance beyond the water hole when they heard the faint rattle of distant gunfire. Bridger and Kingston exchanged glances, but they did not pull up or look around.

Carrie was riding beside Sampson. She turned in

her saddle and looked back at the two men. "You can't be sure, can you?" she taunted them. "You can't be sure that Sands has killed Fargo."

Kingston did not reply, nor did Bridger.

"I think Fargo just killed the sheriff," she said. "And soon he'll be after both of you. You'll never get that gold now. Or if you do, you'll never get it out of these mountains."

"Shut up," snapped Bridger.

"Why should I? I like to see filth like you squirm."

Kingston spurred his horse alongside Carrie's and with a vicious backhand slap sent the girl tumbling off her horse.

Sampson pulled up and jumped down beside her. Kneeling beside the girl, he helped her to a sitting position, then looked up at Kingston and Bridger, his eyes blazing with fury. "If any one of you touches this girl again, I'll take you nowhere but to hell. And that's a promise!"

Kingston took out his six-gun, cocked it, and aimed it down at Sampson's upturned face. "You'll do as we say, old man. And you'll keep that slut of yours silent."

Sampson got quickly to his feet, reached up, and dragged Kingston off his horse. Slamming Kingston to the hard ground, he kicked the six-gun out of his hand. Then he reached down and hauled the astonished gambler to his feet and slapped him so hard the man's eyes rolled back in his head.

"Who you callin' a slut, you son of a bitch," Sampson growled. Then he flung the man back so hard, he tripped and went down.

A shot rang out. Sampson glanced up and saw Bridger, still in his saddle, a smoking gun in his hand. He had fired into the air. His face was scarlet.

"You seem to forget who's in charge here, Sampson."

Ignoring Bridger, Sampson reached down and helped the stunned Carrie to her feet. Then he helped her back into her saddle and mounted up himself.

Only then did Sampson reply. "And you seem to forget who's leading this expedition. You won't find any gold unless I take you to it."

Scrambling to his feet, Kingston glared up at Sampson. "I ain't going to forget that, old man."

"Good," Sampson replied. "I want you to remember it. Next time, maybe you'll watch your mouth." He turned to Carrie. "You all right?"

"Yes. I'm sorry I started that." A thin line of blood was coming from the side of her mouth.

"Never mind that."

Without waiting for Kingston to step into his saddle, Sampson rode out ahead of the other two.

The stream Sampson had promised them was just inside the entrance to Diablo Canyon. They pulled up before it, watered the animals, and filled their canteens. That done, Sampson mounted up. Ahead of him, the floor of the canyon was as clean as a tabletop. There was no sign to follow. Still, Sampson was not about to let that bother him. He was confident Mullin had hidden the gold in that mine shaft.

"Well, Sampson," Bridger said, pulling up alongside Sampson, "it shouldn't be far from here. Where's that mine shaft?"

"In farther."

"Let's go, then."

Sampson kneed his horse deeper into the canyon. From here on, he planned to stall as much as possible. He had to give Fargo a chance to overtake them—assuming Carrie was right, that he had been able to handle the sheriff.

Sampson wasn't worried all that much about himself. It was Carrie's fate that concerned him. And so far, it looked as if Fargo was their only hope.

For better than two hours they rode, following the canyon's winding, snaking course. The sheer walls occasionally fell away, then closed in once again, their striated faces hanging menacingly over them, the sky but a sliver of bright blue high overhead.

At last they rode into a broad, fairly open stretch, and ahead of them Sampson saw the bleached skeletons of four large animals. The bones were scattered close around a low shoulder of rock, beside which a thin stream trickled. At once Sampson knew these skeletons were the remains of Bart Mullin's mules.

Bridger and Kingston saw them at the same time Sampson did and spurred ahead. Dismounting quickly, eagerly, they inspected the remains. By the time Sampson reached them, Bridger had pulled out of one of the rib cages an Apache arrow.

He held it up for Sampson to see.

"Apache," Sampson acknowledged laconically. "Naratena's band, more than likely."

The four skeletons gleamed cleanly in the bright sun. So clean, in fact, had the bones been picked by this time that not a single fly buzzed over them and not a bird could be seen hopping about within their macabre cages. The haunches were missing, and that made sense. The Apaches were not going to pass up fresh meat, even if it were mule.

Kingston looked up at Sampson. "We're getting near, old man. That right?"

"I guess we are at that," Sampson replied, nodding. "Them's Mullin's mules, what's left of them."

"So the box canyon should be near here," prompted Bridger.

"Reckon so."

"Dammit! You should know that for sure," insisted Kingston. "Quit this stalling and lead us to it."

With a weary shrug, Sampson urged his horse around the pile of bones and led the way deeper into Diablo Canyon, Carrie keeping close by him. Kingston and Bridger promptly mounted up and followed them. As he rode, Sampson's eyes searched the canyon's rims on either side.

Where in hell is Fargo? he wondered. Can that bear of a man have let the sheriff kill him?

From the canyon rim, Fargo watched. Sampson could not see him because Fargo was keeping well back from the rim as he rode, content to dismount only occasionally to make sure the four were still below him. He had overtaken them a few miles before they discovered the mules' remains, and while they were inspecting them, he had ridden a half a mile or so ahead, looking for a spot where he could make his move.

He found what he was looking for when he came upon a place in the canyon where it narrowed to a bottleneck that would allow at best only three horses to ride abreast. Dismounting, he tied up his pinto, and armed only with the big Colt he had liberated from the sheriff, he slanted down the steep slope. He was doing fine until a fissure opened before him, blocking his progress. He lowered himself cautiously into it. Then, keeping close to the layered red rocks, he jumped from ledge to ledge, dropping steadily toward the shadowed canyon floor.

Abruptly, the draw spilled out onto a ledge. At this point, the canyon twisted sharply back, the ledge thrusting out like the prow of a ship. Kneeling on the edge of it, Fargo peered over. Below the ledge there was a shallow pool fed by an anemic stream.

In full flood, this nearly dormant stream came alive with a vengeance, Fargo realized, undoubtedly generating considerable force as it swept against the cliff wall below him. Facing that swift impact of water over the ages, the wall was now deeply undercut, forming a great open-faced cavern. Sizable blocks and slabs of rust-colored rocks had broken off the cliff face and tumbled into the pool and onto the canyon floor near the bend of the stream.

The drop from the ledge was better than sixty feet, too far for him to be sure he would not injure himself if he tried to make it. Fargo retreated from the ledge and worked his way along it until he found a crack in the canyon wall as broad as a roadway, slanting down toward the canyon floor. Fargo could not tell how far it went, but he had no choice now.

He picked his way down through the crack in the rock face until he was confronted by five- or six-foot fissure that ran at a right angle to the crack. He would have to leap over it to keep going. He backed up, raced to the edge of the fissure, and jumped. But he had not been able to generate enough momentum in the narrow space and fell short. He caught himself with his forearms, cracking them smartly, then hauled himself out and continued on down the crack.

Not long after, the crack gave out and he found himself directly under the ledge he had peered down from a moment before. The drop from this height was much less than from the other ledge, but it was still at least fifteen feet, and the ground around that shallow pool was littered with those broken slabs of rock he had noticed from above.

Still, he had no choice. He crawled out onto the lip and lowered himself over the edge. He hung for a moment, looking down through his boots at two large, ugly hunks of rust-colored boulders just beneath him. He would have to land beyond them. He swung himself outward, then back in, and did this until he had generated enough momentum. The loose rock and grit was cutting into his palms by this time, and he was forced to drop before he was ready.

Fortunately, he only grazed the worst of the rocks and sprawled facedown in the cool, shadowed sand under the ledge. Picking himself up, he unholstered his Colt and raced back to the narrow bottleneck in the canyon and hunkered down behind a clump of scrub pine. By this time, Sampson and his party were only fifteen to twenty yards farther down the canyon.

Sampson was in the lead, Carrie riding alongside. He was pleased to see her riding on the inside. Behind them rode Kingston and Bridger, the mules trailing them. As he rode, Sampson was peering intently around him at the canyon walls.

Fargo wasn't worried about Sampson. In a pinch the old prospector could take care of himself, he was sure. But Fargo's first task, as he saw it, was to snatch Carrie out of Bridger's and Kingston's clutches. Only then could Sampson and he take them on. There was little doubt in Fargo's mind that Carrie's vulnerability was the reason Sampson had gone along with those two for as long as he had.

Fargo waited, praying that nothing would change the course the four riders were taking, and that Carrie would remain as close as she was now to the canyon wall. At last, the shadow of Carrie's mount fell over him. Reaching up swiftly, he grabbed Carrie about the waist and dragged her down beside him.

"My horse is up on the ridge," he told her. "I'll cover you."

Then he pushed her down the trail. She glanced back at him, her face a pale, astonished flower in the shadow of the canyon wall.

"Go on!"

She turned and ran off like a spooked deer.

Fargo swung around then and brought up his six-gun. But before he could get off a shot, Bridger's horse drove into him, slamming him back against the wall. Fargo tried to shoot up at Bridger, but the crushing pressure of the startled, rearing horse caused his shot to go wild. Before he could fire again, Kingston hurled himself off his horse onto Fargo's back, his weight bearing Fargo to the ground.

As the two men struggled, Fargo saw Bridger pull his horse back and train his revolver on Sampson to keep the old man from going to Fargo's aid. Suddenly, Kingston managed to crack Fargo smartly on the skull with his six-gun. The effect was devastating. Dropping his own gun, Fargo felt himself slump loosely to the ground.

Kingston picked up Fargo's gun and passed it up to Bridger, who stuck it into his belt. Then, stepping back, Kingston stood over Fargo for a moment, enjoying the spectacle of Fargo twisting on the ground in silent agony. Then he kicked Fargo viciously in the side.

"You must forgive me, Mr. Fargo," Kingston said, chuckling, "but that kick has been such a long time coming, and it gives me great satisfaction." He holstered his weapon.

After a moment, the throbbing in Fargo's head abated enough to enable him to haul himself painfully to his feet.

Bridger moved his horse closer and peered coldly down at him. "That was foolish, Fargo. Where's that girl going to find help in a wilderness like this?"

Fargo didn't bother to reply.

Kingston spoke up then. "Where's the sheriff?"

Fargo ran his hand through his hair and remained silent.

Kingston chuckled. "Hell, Fargo must've killed the son of a bitch," he told Bridger. "He wouldn't be here if he hadn't. Looks like we got one less person to share this gold with."

"You ain't got it yet," said an aroused Sampson, obviously unhappy he had not been able to help Fargo during the struggle.

Bridger turned on him. "I wouldn't take that tack," he warned. "I swear, if you do, Sampson, we'll just take you apart like an old clock."

"What'll we do with Fargo?" Kingston asked.

Bridger shrugged. "Whatever you suggest."

"I say we use him to load up that gold. I want to see the son of a bitch sweat. And then, when we're finished with him, I want to see the bastard crawl."

"Get onto the girl's horse, Fargo," said Bridger.

Fargo mounted up. The dizziness had abated and he had no difficulty sitting the horse. He put it alongside Sampson's and they continued on down the canyon, the other two keeping right behind them.

*　　*　　*

Not long after, Sampson pointed out an arroyo to Fargo. "We go through there," he told him.

"What's that, Sampson?" Kingston demanded, spurring alongside.

"I told him we're going through that arroyo. The box canyon's on the other side."

"That's more like it, old man."

"Damn you," Sampson exploded. "Don't keep calling me an old man."

Kingston just laughed and pulled his horse back.

The arroyo was so narrow they had to ride through it single-file. Its floor dropped rapidly under them as red dirt and loose rock showered down whenever they brushed the walls. Finally, the arroyo spilled out onto a sloping, massive cap rock. A few hundred yards or so ahead of them, the canyon made a sharp turn to the right.

Sampson spoke up then, grudgingly. "The mine shaft should be behind that turn."

"It better be," said Bridger from behind them. "Or it'll be your hide."

Fargo and Sampson clattered across the cap rock, the other two surging abreast of them, glancing eagerly forward as they rode. Their lust for the gold was like an unpleasant smell they were giving off.

When at last they made the turn, Sampson and Fargo were a little behind the two. Sampson looked up at the canyon walls on both sides. Fargo heard the man gasp softly.

"What is it?" he asked Sampson.

"I could have sworn," he whispered.

"Something wrong?"

Sampson pulled up hastily. "The mine shaft," he replied hoarsely. "It's not here. It's gone."

11

The moment Sampson pulled up, Bridger and Kingston did the same. Then they hauled their mounts around and galloped back to Sampson. Both men knew from the look on Sampson's face that something was wrong—and they didn't like it.

"Where's that mine entrance?" Kingston demanded.

"I'm not sure."

"Goddammit! Talk plain. What are you telling us?"

"I'm telling you I don't know where the mine shaft is. It was supposed to be here, but it's . . . gone!"

Bridger whipped out his six-gun and clubbed Sampson off his horse. As Sampson struck the ground, Fargo launched himself at Bridger. The man struck the ground underneath Fargo, and Fargo managed to get a few quick, sledging blows to his face before Kingston clubbed him from behind again.

Despite the pain and the sudden weakness in his knees, Fargo managed to stay upright and turn on Kingston. But Kingston was holding the muzzle of his six-gun only inches from Fargo's chest.

"Go ahead, Fargo," Kingston said, smiling. "Go ahead. Take another step toward me. Make me use this."

Fargo held up.

Sampson tried to get up. Bridger stepped forward and kicked him in the side of the head, sending the old man flopping over onto his back. A two-inch laceration opened across his right cheekbone.

"Now, you listen here," Bridger said, bending over Sampson. "We let you get away with your insolence back there. But we're in this here box canyon you been tellin' us about. So quit stalling or I'll leave you here for the buzzards."

Sampson pushed himself to a sitting position and glared venomously up at Bridger. "Do to me what you want, you son of a bitch. The entrance to that mine shaft is gone."

Bridger straightened up, his eyes cold. "Get up."

Slowly, painfully, Sampson got to his feet.

"Now let's hear that again," Bridger said.

Wearily, Sampson pointed to the canyon wall on his right. "There should be a clean rock face there. And where the entrance to the mine should be, there's all them boulders piled up. Maybe there's been an avalanche. Either that or this here ain't the right canyon."

Bridger and Kingston exchanged glances. They were obviously dismayed. They could not be sure if Sampson was stalling them or not. But what they knew for certain was that they were no closer to the gold they coveted than they had been when they started out.

Licking his lips nervously, Bridger said to Sampson, "Well, what do you suggest?"

"It might be a good idea to keep going. Maybe there's another bend in this here canyon farther down. I might be mixed up, is all."

Bridger glanced at Kingston. Kingston nodded. "All right," said Bridger, turning back to Sampson. "Mount up. We'll keep going."

"Fargo," snapped Kingston, "take the lead on these mules."

Fargo reached back for the reins, then spurred alongside Sampson. Sampson glanced at him and Fargo saw the desperation in the old man's eyes. In order to save both their lives, he was stalling. Sampson had no idea where in hell that mine shaft had disappeared to, and once those two behind him realized that for sure, they would simply put a bullet in both of them and light out.

Ahead of them Fargo saw another arroyo opening off the canyon. This one was a bit wider than the other one, but not much more so. He glanced at Sampson, then pointed.

Sampson nodded, eyes narrowing. Then he winked at Fargo. Clearing his throat, he glanced past Fargo at Bridger and Kingston. "Ahead of us," he said, "that arroyo. I think I recognize that now. Maybe it's through there."

"Damn you, old man," said Kingston, "if this is another one of your tricks, you won't ride out of here alive."

"It looks familiar. Hell, these canyons are like a maze. You know how easy it is to get lost in them."

"Maybe so," said Bridger, hope creeping into his voice as he spurred closer.

"You want us to go in first?" Sampson asked.

"Yeah. And don't try nothin'," said Kingston. "We'll be right behind you."

They reached the arroyo, a deep cleft in an otherwise solid wall of rock. Sampson glanced quickly back at Fargo, to make sure they were both thinking the same thing. This time it was Fargo who winked. Sampson suddenly spurred his horse into the arroyo, Fargo staying right behind him as he dragged the four mules after him.

As the cool, shadowed walls of the draw closed over Fargo, he heard Kingston's shout. Dropping the mules reins, he left the four beasts behind and spurred after Sampson. Glancing back, he saw the mules milling confusedly in the narrow passageway, effectively blocking Bridger and Kingston.

A shot rang out, its echo filling the draw with its thunder. As the round ricocheted past him, Fargo lowered his head and kept going. He was nearly out of the arroyo when he looked back once more and saw Kingston's horse attempting to push its way through the tight-packed mules. Whinnying in confusion, it reared suddenly, its front legs pawing at the air, and Kingston went tumbling backward off the animal, which lurched over onto him, struggling frantically. Behind Kingston,

Bridger was desperately attempting to drive through the milling burros and past Kingston's thrashing horse.

As Fargo galloped out of the arroyo, he saw Sampson rein in a few yards ahead of him. Overtaking Sampson, Fargo saw what had stopped him. They were on a ledge. Below it, a great fissure—a ragged rip in the earth's mantle—cut down through the layered red rock toward the shadowed depths of what appeared to be another canyon.

The drop to the floor of that canyon was better than a hundred feet. There was no safe way down, even on foot.

Fargo looked to the slope on his left. It was steep, but navigable. They would have to scramble up on foot. Fargo glanced back into the arroyo. Somehow Bridger had managed to ride around the mules and Kingston's downed horse. He was urging his horse on through the draw at almost a gallop.

"There's no other way," Fargo told Sampson as he dismounted. "Let's get up that slope."

Sampson nodded and dismounted also.

The footing was treacherous. Rocks Fargo needed for support came loose in his grasp. The gravel under his boots gave way. He found himself sliding down the slope almost as often as he made progress up it. Fargo steadied himself and looked back just in time to see Bridger ride out of the draw, shading his eyes as he looked up the slope after them. A second later Kingston appeared behind him.

Both men went for their six-guns.

Fargo looked back at Sampson. He, too, was looking back down the slope at the two men.

"Keep going," Fargo told him. "And keep your ass down."

Sampson turned about and resumed his scrambling climb. A six-gun below them fired. Alongside Fargo's right hand a rock disintegrated. Another gunshot sounded.

Fargo heard the sound of a bullet thunking into solid flesh. Glancing up, he saw Sampson stiffen, reach out haltingly for a tree root, then begin to slide backward. He was rolling by the time he reached Fargo. Fargo reached over and tried to grab him, but Sampson was past him before Fargo could get a hand on him. As Fargo watched in dismay, the old man slid brokenly all the way back down the slope.

Bridger and Kingston then opened up on Fargo. Fargo kept himself flat as the rounds ricocheted around him. He was trapped—like a treed coon on a moonlit night.

Then, from the slope above, a powerful rifle cracked. Astonished, Fargo glanced up and saw Carrie, his Sharps in her hand. Carrie had found the pinto! A howl of pain and surprise came from below him. Looking down, Fargo saw Kingston swing his horse around and duck back into the arroyo. Bridger, his hand grasping at his left shoulder, was roweling furiously after him.

Swiftly, Fargo clawed his way up the slope. When he reached the crest, a flushed, tearful Carrie thrust the Sharps into his hand.

"I wasn't sure how to load it," she cried, "or I would have fired sooner."

"Never mind that. You did fine," he told her. "Where's the pinto?"

"Back here."

She showed Fargo where she had left the Ovaro. It was waiting patiently. Fargo flipped open one of his saddlebags and brought out his box of Sharps cartridges. Dropping a handful into his side pocket, he selected one, reloaded the Sharps, and hurried back to the slope.

Peering down, he saw no sign of Bridger and Kingston. Sampson was lying where he had fallen, his face staring up at them. Fargo plunged down the slope toward him, Carrie scrambling frantically alongside him.

But once they reached Sampson's side, one look was all they needed. The old man was dead.

Wordlessly, Carrie knelt by his body, and bowed over him. She rocked in silent grief, tears coursing down her cheeks. Fargo watched. He felt as miserable as she did, but there was nothing he could say or do. After a moment, he left her and walked into the arroyo.

The mules were still where he had left them, waiting patiently, stupidly, in the shadows—and there was no sign of either Bridger or Kingston. They were long gone, he realized. With Bridger wounded, Sampson dead, and Carrie armed with a Sharps on the ridge above them, there was no longer any reason for them to hang around.

Fargo went back to Carrie. As his shadow fell

147

over her, she looked up at him, tears tracking her face.

"There's a spot . . . back of his cabin," she managed. "Under a cottonwood. He spoke of it to me."

"Then we'll take him there," he said. "Go back up the slope and get the pinto. Meet me in Diablo Canyon. Can you get back to it all right?"

She nodded.

"Okay. I'll meet you there with Sampson's body."

She stood up and without a word to him toiled back up the slope. He watched her go. Once she had disappeared beyond the crest, he set to work lifting the old prospector up onto his horse, then tying him down.

Astride the sheriff's mount, Fargo led the horse carrying Sampson's body and drove the mules ahead of him into Diablo Canyon. He left them near the stream so they would have enough water and graze, and he kept going until Carrie appeared, riding toward him on the Ovaro. They exchanged mounts. It was late in the afternoon by the time they emerged from the canyon.

As they started across the flat beyond the canyon's entrance, Fargo pulled up suddenly to study the tracks left by Bridger and Kingston. It appeared that the two riders had stayed together for only a short while before separating. One rider had veered northeast, toward the mountains and the high plans beyond. The other set of tracks was heading straight back for Gold City.

Carrie glanced at him. "Do you want to go after them?"

He nodded. "After that one heading north. He'll get clean away if he clears them mountains. I think that rider heading for Gold City is Kingston."

"Leave me, then. I can take Sampson back to the cabin."

He handed her the reins. "You understand why I want to do this?"

"Don't you think it's what I want also?" she asked bitterly. "I'd do it myself if I could."

"Wait for me at the cabin."

"All right."

He pulled the pinto around and quickly lifted him to a lope. If he was right, and the rider he was following was Bridger, he was a wounded man and not likely to cover much ground in his condition. In that one glance Fargo had managed from the slope, it appeared to him that Bridger had suffered only a flesh wound in the shoulder. But a man could never tell. That Sharps packed a mean wallop.

Fargo had no trouble following his quarry. Bridger—and by now Fargo was fairly certain this was whom he was trailing—was in such a hurry that he rode straight for the mountains, making no effort at all to hide his trail or shake off any pursuit.

There was an hour of daylight left when Fargo reached the foothills and began lifting into a high, gaunt country, hemmed in by sheer cliffs and scrub-covered buttes and ridges. On the higher elevations there were scattered stands of pine and ash, but mostly the sun-baked land was scarred with mesquite and long stretches of bleached sandstone sticking up through the ground and out of the sides of canyons like enormous bones.

But Bridger's sign was still perfectly clear as the man galloped down the middle of one canyon after another, seemingly intent only on putting distance between himself and any possible pursuers. Considering the pace he was keeping, Fargo no longer felt he was injured at all seriously.

Soon the barren, eroded foothills fell away behind him and Fargo found himself riding across a flat. It was covered for the most part with tough grama grass and was watered by a thin, sluggish stream. Splashing across the stream finally, Fargo saw the clear imprint of Bridger's horse in the soft ground as the fleeing Wells Fargo agent turned his horse somewhat abruptly toward a pine-crowned escarpment north of the flat.

At the same time, Fargo saw the prints of unshod Indian ponies. In this country that could mean only one thing: Apaches. Their tracks appeared as fresh, perhaps even fresher, than those left by Bridger's mount.

Fargo urged the Ovaro to a gallop, his eyes alert to any movement along the top of the ridge. The closer he got to the escarpment, the more formidable and massive it appeared as it lifted into the sky before him. Still following Bridger's tracks, Fargo saw a cleft in the massive rock wall. It yawned steadily wider the closer he got.

And Bridger's tracks were heading on a straight line for it.

He was forced to slow the pinto some in order to

thread his way through the rock-littered ground fronting the cleft. Rounding a particularly hefty boulder, Fargo glanced up at the rim and caught the sudden bright glint of a gun barrel. Ducking low over the pinto's neck, he dug his heels into its flanks. As the horse shot forward, the crack of Bridger's rifle echoed sharply among the rocks, the round ricocheting off among the rocks just behind him. The distant rifle cracked again. Like an angry hornet, a bullet whined past his right shoulder and exploded against the side of a boulder.

A moment later and the pinto had carried him into the shadowed cleft. He found the cleft widening almost to the breadth of an avenue as he clattered on through it. Before long, he had cut completely through the massive ridge and was emerging on its northern face. Flinging himself from the pinto, he snaked his Sharps from its scabbard and angled quickly up the rock-strewn slope toward the rim.

The treacherous footing caused him to slip more than once. The sharp rocks tore into his buckskin pants, drawing blood from his knees. But he paid no attention as he swept on up toward the rim, anxious to outflank the spot where he had caught the glint of sunlight along Bridger's rifle barrel. His hope was to trap the man with his back to the escarpment.

Reaching the crest of the ridge, the Trailsman raced along it, heading toward a towering rock face, from the base of which Bridger's fire had come. Abruptly, the ground began to slope. Fargo found himself leaping from one giant slab of rock to another, each one lower than the one before it. Fargo felt like an undersized human attempting to negotiate the steps of some giant creature.

When he reached a thin spine of sandstone, he followed it toward the rim until his progress was blocked by a precipitous drop. Studying the ground below the drop, he saw it was a narrow game trail studded with scrub pine.

Slowly, handling the Sharps with great care, he began climbing down the almost sheer rock wall to the trail below. He was halfway down, resting on a narrow ledge, when he heard the sound of rapid hoofbeats coming from the rim.

Though he knew it was a gamble, Fargo carefully dropped his rifle to the trail below, aiming for a thick juniper bush on the trail below him. He saw the rifle disappear through the branches and heard it thump to the carpet of pine needles. No longer encumbered by the Sharps, Fargo dropped swiftly and steadily toward the trail below. His hands were bloody when he dropped finally to the trail and caught sight of his rifle a few feet from him.

As he hurried toward it, Bridger galloped into view. He was less than thirty yards away, his horse lathered cruelly under his punishing usage. His left shoulder was dark with dried blood and he was holding the Colt he had taken from Fargo in his right hand, the muzzle pointed directly at him.

Crabbing sideways, Fargo snatched up his rifle just as Bridger fired. The round stuck the rock wall beside Fargo, driving tiny rock shards into his face.

Flinching away, Fargo fired the Sharps from his hip. The slug pounded into the horse's chest. The horse sprawled, sending Bridger tumbling forward over his neck.

Bridger landed like a cat, shook himself, then came erect, the six-gun still clutched in his hand. The horse, struggling desperately, lurched wildly to its feet, brushing against Bridger as it ran off. As Bridger stumbled momentarily forward, Fargo unsheathed his bowie and charged him. Ducking to one side, Bridger chopped down on Fargo's head with the six-gun.

The blow to Fargo's still-tender skull was almost instantly disabling. The world rocked about him sickeningly. Again Bridger used the gun barrel, this time to club the bowie from Fargo's hand. Somehow Fargo managed to stay on his feet, and with the sullen, brute determination of a wounded bull, he again charged Bridger. It did not matter to him if Bridger emptied his revolver into him, Fargo was going to claw Bridger to the ground and then close his ten fingers around the man's scrawny neck.

Bridger fired. The round snicked past Fargo's shoulder—and a moment later Fargo had slammed Bridger back against a rock face. Fargo heard Bridger gasp, then reached up for his throat. Dropping his six-gun, Bridger clawed away Fargo's tightening fingers and managed to spin away from the still-unsteady Fargo. Snatching up his gun, he stepped quickly out of Fargo's reach and aimed point-blank at Fargo.

Fargo ignored the weapon in Bridger's hand and charged again.

Like tiny black thunderbolts, two Apache arrows plunged out of the sky and buried themselves in Bridger's back. The sound their passage made was like the whisper of wings. As the man collapsed to his knees, a third arrow sank into his back. Without a sound, Bridger toppled forward onto his face. As he did so, a final arrow buried itself in his back.

Straightening, Fargo glanced around him.

An Apache had already stepped out from the rocks to his right. He stood there silently, gazing impassively at Fargo. Another Apache stepped into view, then a third. As if by magic, more Apaches began materializing from the rocks, until there were close to a dozen silent Apaches surrounding him.

Fargo recognized two of the Indians at once.

The unusually tall Apache with a white headband and piercing blue eyes was Naratena. The Indian who stood beside him was the Zuni medicine man who had nursed Fargo back to life.

Naratena stepped closer to Fargo.

"Looks like this is the second time I owe you," Fargo acknowledged.

"You would have killed him. His bullets would not have been able to stop you. But this man killed Old White Beard. For this we kill him." Naratena indicated the dead Bridger with a glance. "But why was such a man brought to the Apaches' golden mountain by Old White Beard? Why did the old one do this?"

"This one and two others forced him," Fargo

said. "They wanted the gold Bart Mullin hid in that mine shaft." Fargo shrugged. "But Sampson could not find it."

Naratena looked shrewdly at Fargo. "That hole in the mountain. It is gone. Do you not remember, One Who Moves Mountains?"

Fargo frowned. Why in hell should *he* remember?

The old Zuni stepped closer and peered up at Fargo with bright black eyes. "In the night," he said, his voice a dusty whisper, "when you join warriors. Think back."

As Fargo looked into the Zuni's face, he felt a host of dim memories shake loose within him. Still, this only confused him further. Was he remembering what had happened—or was he simply recalling the fearsome nightmares that had ridden through his disordered sleep those many long nights?

The Zuni spoke again, his voice prodding. "You called out to the White Painted Woman and Child of Water. Then you fell upon the mountain and tore it loose. You sent a great piece of it down to cover the hole the miners dug. Do you not remember this? We danced until the stars fled. Your medicine was powerful that night."

Fargo remembered.

The confusion of images became clear at last. He felt again the ledge trembling under his feet as he sent that great boulder crashing down into the night. He recalled, too, the sweating, heaving bodies of the Apaches who had joined him in his labor. And with this memory he realized why Sampson

155

had been unable to find the entrance to the mine shaft. Fargo himself had led the Apaches in obliterating it.

Fargo smiled at the Zuni. "Your medicine is powerful, too." Then he looked back at Naratena. "But others will come for that gold. They will dig through those rocks and debris and take it back with them. It belongs to Wells Fargo."

Naratena frowned. "And who is this Wells Fargo?"

"It is a company of men who send their gold through your land to California in their stagecoaches."

"Tell this Wells Fargo Naratena will keep the gold. And tell him the hole in the mountain is closed forever to the white eyes—but not to the Apache. With these bricks of gold Naratena will buy much from the Comancheros, many wagon guns, many rifles and bullets."

"But if you take that gold, you would be stealing it from Wells Fargo—just as Mullin and his gang did."

Naratena appeared genuinely mystified by Fargo's insistence on this. "Why not I take this gold back?" he asked. "It belongs to the Apache. It is from our mountains the gold comes. And now this Wells Fargo he bring it back to us—a gift to the Apache for letting him drive his stagecoach through our land."

"You mean you will allow Wells Fargo to do that?"

"Yes."

"And you will no longer attack the Wells Fargo way stations?"

Naratena scowled. "Apache not burn station. Mullin and his men do this. He kill and burn his own people. He do this so white eyes think it is Apache who kill and burn."

Fargo took a deep breath. His hunch had been right. It made sense. How many of Mullin's assorted depredations had been blamed on the Apaches? he wondered. If this gold shipment had been successfully raised by Mullin, it would probably have been blamed on the Apaches.

"All right," Fargo agreed. "I will tell Wells Fargo what Naratena has said."

Naratena nodded, satisfied. "And will the One Who Moves Mountains see to that other white eyes who kill Old White Beard? We see him flee to Gold City."

Fargo wondered if there was anything that happened in these mountains that these Apaches did not know of. Probably not.

"I will see to that one," Fargo told the chief.

"Good," said Naratena. "I am content. Leave the Golden Mountains now. They shall bleed no more for the white eyes. Tell this to all the other white eyes. But for you, the One Who Moves Mountain, there will be bricks of gold. How many will you take?"

"None," Fargo replied. "It is Apache gold, after all. There is already too much blood on it."

Naratena studied Fargo's face intently for a moment, then nodded. He understood. "Then go.

The Apache will not hinder your passage through his land.''

Fargo walked over to Bridger's sprawled corpse, picked his Colt up off the ground, then walked over to pick up his Sharps. When he glanced up again, the Apaches were gone.

12

It was late that night when Fargo reached Sampson's cabin. A large pale moon hung over the flat before it. Yellow lantern light filled the two windows. Carrie had made it back all right.

She was standing in the open doorway when he pulled to a halt.

"Everything okay?" he asked as he dismounted.

"Yes," she said, and walked out to join him as he led the pinto into the barn. She watched silently while he unsaddled the pinto, rubbed him down, and then fed and watered him. She was still silent when they slumped finally, wearily, down at the kitchen table.

Her hands clasped before her, she looked with wide, unhappy eyes at Fargo. They were swollen from crying, and she looked pale and drawn. She had really loved the old man.

"Bridger's dead," he told her.

"Good," she said, her eyes suddenly bright with venom.

"The Apaches took a hand in it. They knew it was Bridger killed Sampson."

"Does that mean you are going to let Kingston live?"

Her cold, frightening need to see Kingston die as well was somewhat unnerving. But then no one had ever been able to convince Fargo that it was only the milk of human kindness that flowed in a woman's veins. He had seen where there was no harder place in God's universe than a woman's breast.

"No, it does not."

"When will you go after him?"

"I need sleep," Fargo said wearily, not wanting to answer her directly.

"Then sleep."

He nodded, pushed himself erect, and started for Sampson's bedroom.

"No," she said. "He's in there."

Pulling up in the doorway, he glanced into the room and saw the dim figure of Sampson Riley lying faceup in the darkness. It gave Fargo a momentary qualm.

"In my bed," Carrie said. "You can sleep there."

Without a word, Fargo turned into her bedroom and dropped like a tree onto the bed. He felt her pulling off his boots, then dropping a blanket over him. When she crawled in beside him, he put his arms around her and held her close. She needed comforting, he realized. Needed it desperately. She began to weep silently, her fragile shoulder shuddering. He held her close and stroked her hair wordlessly. After a long while she slept.

Only then did Fargo allow himself to fall asleep.

The next morning they buried Sampson under the cottonwood behind the cabin he had mentioned to her, then set out for Gold City. It was late in the afternoon when they rode into it. Fargo got a room for them both at the hotel, then left Carrie and headed for the express office.

The mining town was in its usual uproar with draymen cursing their overloaded teams, carriages clogging the streets, miners and assorted types swarming in and out of the saloons. There was so much activity when Fargo and Carrie rode in that few had noticed them. Now, only a few appeared to recognize Fargo as he headed down the wooden walk toward the express office—and those few who did were careful to say nothing as they stepped out of Fargo's path.

As Fargo mounted the porch fronting the Wells Fargo office, Skip Turpin appeared in the office doorway.

"Afternoon, Skip," Fargo said to the astonished clerk.

Skip was dressed in clean pants and vest, a white shirt of good-quality broadcloth under it. He stood a mite taller, it seemed. But his astonishment at seeing Fargo was as genuine as ever.

"Mr. Fargo!"

"That's right, Skip. In the flesh. I keep turning up, don't I?"

"You sure do, but I'm right glad to see you."

161

"Thanks," Fargo said, pausing in front of Skip. "You sure look mighty prosperous."

"I'm the new Wells Fargo agent," Skip was smiling proudly.

"Kind of a fast promotion, wasn't it?"

"Guess maybe it was," Skip admitted, blushing. "But I'm sure I can handle it, Mr. Fargo."

"I am, too."

At that moment a short, stocky fellow with long sideburns and a thick, bushy mustache strode out of the office and paused beside Skip. He was dressed in a fine pin-striped navy-blue suit and a black fedora. His pants legs were stuffed carelessly into beautifully tooled boots.

"This here's Silas Worthington," Skip told Fargo. "He's a Pinkerton man, working for Wells Fargo."

Worthington allowed himself a brief smile and stuck out his hand. Fargo shook it.

"So you're this one I been hearing about. Skye Fargo."

"Reckon so."

"Shall we go inside?" Worthington suggested.

Fargo and Skip followed Worthington into the office. Skip closed the door behind them as Fargo and Worthington entered the inner office.

"All right, mister," Worthington said, thumbing his fedora back off his forehead. "What can you tell me about that gold shipment?"

"Wells Fargo will never see it again."

"That so?"

"The agent here, Bridger, is dead. He conspired with Mullin to rob the shipment. Slade Kingston, a local gambler, and the sheriff were in on it with him."

Worthington nodded. "I know all that. One of our agents sent here more than a few weeks ago already informed our office in San Francisco. His name was Carl Renstadt. He was posing as a whiskey drummer."

"Yes, I know."

"I understand he was on that stage, the one that was robbed."

"He was."

"And Mullin's gang killed him?"

"The sheriff liquored him up—probably slipped something into his booze—then piled Renstadt onto the stage before we pulled out. From the looks of it, Mullin knew what to do with Renstadt when he raised the stage. It was very neat."

"Do you have any idea where the sheriff is now?"

"He's dead."

"And Bridger?"

"Sleepin' with four Apache arrows in his back."

Skip cleared his throat. The young man was obviously eager to get Fargo up to date. "Mr. Fargo," he spoke up, "Slade Kingston's at the Miner's Haven. Ever since he got back, he's been doin' some talkin'. He said you murdered the sheriff and Bridger."

"Does he now?"

"And the town marshal has a warrant for your arrest."

"On what charge?"

"Killing Rex Barry."

"They found his body outside of town, then."

Skip nodded.

"Does anyone really believe I killed Rex?"

"I don't think so. But you must know how they feel about you, breaking out like that. And killing that miner who tried to draw on you."

"I was supposed to have let him cut me down. Is that it?"

"Hell, Mr. Fargo, I know you done the only thing you could to save yourself. I was there. And everyone else knew that too, once they got thinkin' on it. The way I see it, a lot of people around here are pretty ashamed of what happened that night."

"But the town marshal still has that warrant?"

Skip nodded gloomily. "It was sworn out right after they found Rex's body."

"Well, I'll let the marshal do what he thinks is best. Then I'll do what I think is best."

Worthington cleared his throat. "Mr. Fargo, if you don't mind, I would like to return to the subject of that gold shipment. Would you explain what you meant when you said Wells Fargo will never see it again?"

"They won't. The Apaches have it." Fargo smiled thinly. "Naratena, their chief, would like me to thanks Wells Fargo for returning the gold to him. He accepts it as a gift—and as payment for letting Wells Fargo use that route through the mountains."

"And you actually believe that the Apache will abide by that bargain?"

"I do."

"You look like a man who has more sense than

that, Fargo. Are you forgetting that this is the same Apache chieftain who has already burned down one of our way stations and killed the station master and his family?"

"That was Bart Mullin's work. His plan was to cover this raise by blaming it on an Apache uprising. It might have worked, too, if he had been able to get away with the gold. It is easy to blame everything on the Apache in this country. Maybe too easy."

"Then you're certain this harassment of our stages and way stations will cease? The Apaches will not bother Wells Fargo's stages?"

Fargo nodded. "For now, anyway."

"Well, dammit, that's good news. I am sure the Wells Fargo office in San Francisco will be glad to get this news. And you say this chief is keeping the gold?"

"Yes."

"I didn't think the aborigines understood the value of gold."

"This one does."

"Well, he's welcome to it, I'd wager—if he keeps his promise. Of course, I can't really speak for Wells Fargo." Worthington sighed and leaned back in his chair. "Now, about this other fellow, Kingston. You say he was in this with Bridger."

Fargo nodded.

"Do you have any evidence? If you do, perhaps I could help in his apprehension. If he had anything to do with Carl Renstadt's death, I would be most eager to do so."

"I'd prefer you leave him to me."

The Pinkerton shrugged. "If you wish."

Fargo got to his feet and looked at Skip. "You said Kingston's in the Miner's Haven?"

"That's right, Mr. Fargo."

"Thanks."

As Fargo reached the door, the Pinkerton called out softly, "Good hunting, Mr. Fargo."

Word of Fargo's return had long since reached the saloon, and at least two patrons had hurried to Kingston's table to whisper the news to him. Kingston had nevertheless remained at the poker table, determined not to run this time. That he had lit out from the canyon with Bridger still nettled him. Now he would stand and fight. Fortunately, he had left nothing to chance. Fargo would be dead and Kingston would be in the clear. And with Fargo gone, there would be no one left who could point an accusing finger at him concerning the stage holdup.

The grizzled miner sitting across from Kingston was looking unhappily at his cards. Kingston waited patiently for him to bet. Everyone in the saloon—the place was as still as death now—was waiting along with Kingston.

Blinking unhappily across the table at Kingston, the miner bet

Kingston met his bet and raised it.

Trapped, the miner looked helplessly about, then pushed his few remaining chips into the pot. "That's all I got," he said. "I'll owe you."

"Yes, you will," said Slade.

"You callin' me?"

"I am."

The miner showed his three kings.

Slade spread his full house on the table for the miner to inspect, then reached over casually and pulled in the pot. "Give your IOU to the barkeep," Slade said to the miner as he carried the chips over to the bar.

As the barkeep paid him off, Slade looked about at the patrons. Every eye was on him. Suddenly he smiled. "Drinks on me," he told them.

With a roar the men rushed up to the bar. Slade Kingston buying! It was unheard of and they intended to make the most of it. As the men jockeyed for places at the bar, Slade pushed well away from it, then turned to watch the miners. They were like swine at a trough.

He pushed out of the saloon and hurried across the street to the town marshal's office.

With grim amusement Fargo noticed how the streets and sidewalks of Gold City had almost emptied since his arrival only an hour or so earlier. Those few he met as he strode along the boardwalk swiftly averted their gaze.

When Fargo saw the husky, black-browed fellow advancing diagonally across the street toward him, he at first paid no heed, until he saw the dusty star pinned to his bib overalls, and the newly polished ivory-handled Colt swelling his holster. This, then, would be the town marshal, the one Skip told him had a warrant for his arrest.

Fargo paused on the boardwalk and waited for the town marshal to reach him.

The man stopped a few feet from the walk. Moistening dry lips, he said, "You're under arrest, Mr. Fargo."

"For what?"

"For murdering Rex Barry."

"You believe that, do you?"

"That ain't the point. I got a warrant."

On both sides of the street, a thin wedge of spectators crept closer.

"What's your name, Marshal?" Fargo asked.

"Standish," he said nervously. "I was the blacksmith in town, but I've been the town marshal since the sheriff took after you."

"You sure that's what he did?"

The fellow straightened up, obviously aware that every eye in the town was focused on him now. "You better come along with me."

"Do you have proof I killed Rex, Marshal?"

The man shifted his feet uncertainly.

"How about witnesses?"

The blacksmith moistened his lips again. "I don't care about that. I got this warrant. That's all I need."

Fargo smiled thinly. "Is Slade Kingston your witness? Is he the one who prodded you into coming out here after me?"

The town marshal appeared to hesitate. Then he nodded grudgingly.

"You must want to keep that star awful bad, Standish," Fargo commented wryly.

The blacksmith's eyes narrowed—possibly to make some suitable reply—then widened in sudden, startled surprise. At the same moment Fargo heard Carrie's warning cry from a hotel window above them. His right hand clawing for leather, Fargo spun around and dived to his right just as Slade Kingston fired at him from the mouth of an alley.

The town marshal clutched at his thigh and staggered back, then collapsed to the street. The bullet meant for Fargo had found the blacksmith instead.

As Fargo crabbed swiftly to the right, another round exploded the dust in front of him. Flinging a shot at Kingston, Fargo charged to his feet and bolted up onto the boardwalk, scattering the spectators. He flung another shot at Kingston, the round splitting a shingle inches from Slade's face. The gambler turned and disappeared into the alley.

Fargo raced into the alley after Kingston, saw him turn down the alley that paralleled Main Street. Fargo darted back to the boardwalk, ran past three stores, then barged through a narrow saloon and out its rear door into the back alley. Kingston was just ahead of him, racing toward the rear entrance to the livery stable.

Pulling up quickly, Fargo aimed and fired. Slade stumbled and almost went down. But he regained his balance and ducked into the livery. Fargo raced down the alley and into the stable after him. He froze beside the door, listening. There were no horses in this portion of the stable, he noticed. But the place was unnaturally silent, as if the beams, the loft, the stalls, even the smell of the place were holding its breath along with him, waiting for the first sound.

It came from Fargo's right, the sound of a foot

disturbing fresh hay as it moved restlessly back into a stall. His gun held warily in front of him, Fargo glided cautiously toward the sound. Before he reached the stall, Kingston stepped out of it. In his dangling right hand he held his pearl-handled revolver. His face was white with pain, and from the amount of blood staining his shirtfront, Fargo guessed his bullet must have entered low in Kingston's back and come out just under the rib cage.

Despite the fact that Kingston remained on his feet, he was already a dead man.

"Drop it, Slade," Fargo told him.

"I'm a dead man, Fargo," Kingston said, his voice a hoarse rasp. "You've blown out my back. Why should I be afraid of you now?"

As he spoke, he brought up the gleaming six-gun. Fargo did not hesitate. Thumb-cocking rapidly, he punched two quick rounds into Kingston's chest.

The force of the slugs slammed Slade back. His heels caught on a low pile of freshly piled straw and horse manure. He sat down heavily in it, then doggedly brought up his six-gun. Fargo thumb-cocked, sighted carefully down his barrel, and fired. This bullet caught Slade high in the chest, knocking him back against the side of the stall.

Slade looked surprised. But with the remarkable persistence of a truncated worm, he attempted for the third time to bring up his revolver. Stepping forward swiftly, Fargo kicked the gun out of his hand. At that, the fire died in Slade's eyes, to be replaced by the dark, terrible fear of death. He coughed raggedly as blood bubbled through his lips.

Then he died, sliding down the side of the stall until his face was resting in the manure, a swarm of fat blue flies already buzzing about his head. With the toe of his boot, Fargo tipped the gambler over onto his back. As Kingston came to rest, a bright shuffle of bloodstained playing cards spilled out of a special pocket sewn into his vest.

With a pile of horse manure for a pillow, Slade Kingston lay among aces and kings, revealing at last in death what he had been all his life—a four-flusher and a cheat.

Fargo became aware of men running into the stable and crowding close about him to get a better view of the corpse. Turning abruptly, he pushed roughly through them and out of the livery, striding along purposefully, refusing to reply to those who insisted on congratulating him, anxious only to escape the stench of death.

As Fargo stood by the window in the dark hotel room and looked down at the street, Carrie left the bed and padded softly up behind him. Hugging his waist, she pressed her nakedness against him and rested her cheek against his back.

"I'm sorry," she said. "I didn't mean to be such a nag."

"Forget it."

"I won't ask you to come back to Texas with me again."

He rested his big hands over hers and leaned back against her. "Is that a promise?"

"Yes." She kissed his back lightly. "That's a promise."

He turned around and gazed down into her upturned face. "It's like I said, Carrie. You have a life to resume among your own people. When you get off that stagecoach, calmly pick up the pieces of your old life. But remember. No matter what, don't ever tell anyone what happened after the *rurales* took you. After a while, everyone who matters to you will stop asking. And pretty soon it will be as if you had never been gone."

She smiled. "I will do exactly as you say."

He turned then and glanced down at the dark street. "As for me, I have another trail to follow, it seems. That Pinkerton gave me a lead I want to follow up."

"Will you never rest, Fargo?"

"How can I," he replied, a sudden icy edge to his voice, "while there's a chance that two of them are still out there?"

The cold resolve in his voice caused her to tremble slightly. He understood and said nothing.

After a moment she sighed and rested her face against his chest. "Then let's tend to what we have going for us right now," she whispered. "After all, Fargo, my stagecoach won't be pulling out until late tomorrow morning."

He grinned down at her. "You think I can hold up that long, do you?"

She flung her arms around his neck. "You can

try," she said, raising herself up on her tiptoes and leaning hungrily into him.

"It's a deal." He chuckled, lifting her swiftly, easily in his arms and carrying her back over to the bed.

LOOKING AHEAD

**The following is the opening section
from the next novel in the exciting
Trailsman series from Signet:**

**The Trailsman #33
RED RIVER REVENGE**

*1861, the upper Minnesota side
of the Red River of the North . . .*

"You shall be hanged by the neck until you are
dead."

Skye Fargo heard the words circling inside his
head as he peered out of the small, barred window
at the gallows directly outside. He'd seen plenty of
gallows before but he found himself realizing how
much more grim a device it seemed when it waited
for your neck. He eyes moved past the wooden scaf-
folding as the day's last light slid into darkness.
Dawn would come too damn soon, he grunted,
and with it the hangman's noose. Damn, he swore
bitterly. It was all wrong, stupid, unbelievable, like

a bad dream, only it was all too real, the iron bars and the little jail cell proof of that.

His eyes swept the ramshackle buildings beyond the gallows. The town had a name, Big Moose. He wouldn't be forgetting it. They went in for big mistakes. Hanging him would be one of their biggest, one he didn't figure to let them make though he still hadn't a plan on how to stop it. And time was running out. He swore again as he turned from the window and sat down on the narrow cot in the cell, his lips a thin, tight line. He lay back, his big, powerful, hard-packed frame too large for the cot and felt the frustration and fury balloon up inside him. He was certain of one thing. He wouldn't go walking out into the dawn like a lamb, not for something he hadn't done. At first he thought he was simply being railroaded, made the scapegoat in some kind of conspiracy. But then he began to wonder if they were only doing what they thought was right, all of them, even the girl. She was the key to it, he grunted. They'd believed everything she said. But whether they were cunning or stupid, it didn't change the results any. It was still a noose around his neck.

It had started only three short days ago. Justice in Big Moose was quick when it involved one of the town's important citizens, it seemed. Apparently Sam Ellison was exactly that. Fargo closed his eyes, let his thoughts go back to the very first of it. It was easy enough. It was seared into his mind. He let each moment return, as though it were happening for the first time.

Bur Oak with their gray-brown heavily furrowed bark lined the low ridge as he rode north. He estimated he'd reach Bowdon by sundown without hurrying and he was moving easily when he saw the six horsemen appear, riding hard. They swerved when they saw him, came toward him at a full gallop. An uneasy feeling stabbed at him but he stayed in place and the horsemen drew closer. A heavy-chested man with a square face led the riders, harsh blue eyes under a tan stetson, a face that had seen some fifty years, Fargo guessed. The feeling of uneasiness deepened inside him as the horsemen came to a halt in a half-circle around him. The square-faced man regarded him from under frowning brows and Fargo saw his eyes flick to the glistening Ovaro.

"You're a nervy one, I'll give you that," the man rasped. "You didn't even try to make a run for it."

"Got nothin' to run from," Fargo said evenly.

"You mean you decided you'd no chance to try it," the man flung back.

"What the hell are you talking about?" Fargo frowned.

"You know damn well. Let's have your gun, mister, nice and slow," the man said.

Fargo half-shrugged, seemed to agree as he moved his hand slowly toward his holster when suddenly it became a flash of motion too swift to the eye to follow. The big Colt seemed to leap into his hand and fire all at the same instant and the square-faced man's tan stetson flew from his head as his mouth fell open in astonishment. "The next one makes you a dead man," Fargo growled, his eyes blue-quartz. The man eyed the big Colt, saw it pointed directly at his heart and licked suddenly dry lips. He felt the uncertainty on the part of the other men and forced words through his lips quickly.

"Everybody stays quiet," he said.

"Good advice," Fargo said. His eyes caught the movement to his right and he flicked a glance toward the bur oaks to see the four riders coming through the trees. The first wore a sheriff's silver star on a buckskin vest. He returned his eyes to the square-faced man until the others reached him and he saw the Sheriff held a Remington .44 in his hand.

"Drop the gun, mister," he heard the Sheriff bark.

"You've got it wrong. These six just tried to jump me," Fargo said.

"I said, drop the gun, mister," Fargo heard the Sheriff repeat. "You're under arrest. Drop it."

Fargo let his eyes move to the Sheriff, saw the three men with him had six-guns trained on him. The odds had suddenly been yanked out from under him. His mouth became a thin line as he lowered the Colt, let it slide from his fingers. "What the hell am I under arrest for?" he growled.

"For murdering my foreman," the square-faced

man answered, his voice filled with anger. Fargo gazed at the man as one of the Sheriff's deputies scooped the Colt from the ground and pulled the big Sharps rifle from its saddle holster.

"You're crazy," Fargo snapped.

"We'll let Judge Harrington decide that," Fargo heard the Sheriff answer. "Take him back to Big Moose," the Sheriff said and Fargo saw himself surrounded by the others, herded back along the ridge. Fargo's eyes bored into the Sheriff as the man rode outside the circle of horsemen, a narrow-headed man with a gray mustache and gray strands of hair sticking out from under his belt.

"You've got a name," Fargo called.

"Sheriff Horace Mayberry," the man said, not without pride.

"Well, Sheriff Mayberry, Sir, this is one big damn mistake or one big damn frame-up," Fargo said.

The Sheriff's face darkened in instant anger. "Nobody's framed in my town," he roared.

Fargo returned into silence as the posse rode back with him. Maybe the good sheriff didn't know a frame-up when it happened under his nose, he pondered. He rode in silence, his glance lingering on the square-faced man who rode with a sense of righteous anger. A hard man, he decided, one used to being obeyed, smarter than Sheriff Mayberry, too, he'd wager. "How'd I murder this here foreman of yours, mister?" Fargo asked.

The man turned a hard frown on him. "You

know damn well how you did it. Don't you try to play Sam Ellison for a fool, mister," he said.

"You're a fool or a double-dealing bastard," Fargo commented and saw the man's face flush.

"A hangman's rope will shut that big mouth of yours," Ellison shouted.

Fargo looked away from the man, his own face set in stone. He stayed silent as they rode him into a town with a bank and a main street neater than many he'd seen. The Sheriff halted in front of a structure with two doors, one marked JAIL, the other COURT. "We'll see you here in the morning, Sam," the Sheriff said to Ellison.

"You can count on it," Ellison replied, wheeled away with his five men following.

"Get down," Sheriff Mayberry ordered and Fargo slid from the saddle, found two deputies beside him at once, each holding a gun in his back. He was marched into the doorway marked COURT to find himself in a square room, a double row of chairs at one side and a makeshift judge's bench at the other. A man in a black frock coat sat behind the bench, a tight, puckered-up face and watery blue eyes. "Got him, Fred," the Sheriff said with pride and turned to Fargo. "This here's Judge Fred Harrigan," he informed the big man.

"Can't say I'm delighted," Fargo bit out.

"You've a right to a trial. I'll hold it tomorrow morning," the Judge said. "You're accused of killing Sam Ellison's foreman, Max Twohey. You pleading not guilty?"

"Goddamn right I am," Fargo snapped.

"Let's have your name," the Judge said, taking up a quill pen as he opened a ledger.

"Fargo, Skye Fargo," the big man said. "Some call me the Trailsman." He watched as Judge Harrigan carefully entered the name in the ledger book. "This whole thing is a crock of shit," Fargo said.

The Judge's watery blue eyes glanced up at him. "You'll get a chance to speak your piece come morning," he said. "Meanwhile, you'll be locked in the town jail till then. Take him away."

Fargo felt the two deputies take his arms, turn him and walk him from the court, through a side door and into the jail. Two cells, he saw, and watched as one of the men put his Colt and the big Sharps into a case behind the Sheriff's battered wood desk. "Cell one," Sheriff Mayberry muttered and Fargo was pushed into the first of the cells, a small, square place that had the one virtue of being relatively clean. He saw the Sheriff staring at him, peering hard.

"Got a question?" Fargo said.

"Wondering why you did it," the Sheriff said.

"I didn't do it, goddammit," Fargo flung back.

"They all say that," the Sheriff answered and turned away shaking his head. Fargo's eyes went to the cell door. A heavy lock, he noted unhappily. The Sheriff settled himself behind his desk across the small front room, took up a book and leaned back in a swivel chair. Fargo let himself examine the small cell and found it solid, the window bars all properly imbedded in concrete. He sat down on the narrow cot, still unable to believe what had happened. He frowned in thought and knew the trail wouldn't be going his way. He was being made a scapegoat. But why they'd picked him remained a mystery. Maybe the morning would bring that answer, he grunted, leaned back and drew a deep sigh from the pit of his stomach. He forced himself to relax. There was time yet. Unnecessary worry only sapped a man's strength and cluttered the mind. He was almost as curious as he was angry and he lay down, dozed, woke when the Sheriff changed guard with one of the deputies, a young, blond man who eyed the cell nervously.

Fargo rose when the night was deep, asked for water and waited as the young deputy brought him a big mug. "Stand back from the bars," the man said and Fargo retreated, watched him put the mug on the floor beside the bars and step quickly away. He'd been well trained, Fargo grunted silently as he took the mug in through the bars. The water felt good and he sipped it slowly, lay back on the cot again. He let himself sleep, woke twice to see the deputy asleep in the chair. Fargo swung from the cot on silent footsteps and knelt down at the cell door, examined the lock carefully. Double-bolt, he noted, not the kind he could pick with the point of the throwing knife still strapped to the calf holster around his leg.

He returned to the cot and let himself sleep

through the remainder of the night. He woke to the sound of two deputies and the Sheriff opening the door. One man put a wash basin into the cell while the Sheriff held a rifle on him. They locked the cell door again and Fargo had just finished washing when they returned. "Judge Harrigan's waiting," Sheriff Mayberry said, the rifle held on him again.

Fargo walked between the two deputies, the Sheriff holding the end of the rifle barrel into the small of his back. Inside the small courtroom, Sam Ellison and four of his men sat in the spectator chairs, their faces grim. Fargo was brought to face Judge Harrigan and the Judge pounded his gavel three times, focused his watery-blue eyes on the big man in front of him. "Court's in session," the Judge said. "You've been told the charges against you, Fargo. You got anything to say?"

"Didn't do it. You've got the wrong man," Fargo said.

"What were you doing in this part of the country?" the Judge asked.

"Riding through, on my way north to Bowdon. Got a job waiting there, man by the name of Folsom," Fargo answered.

"Got a written agreement that says so?" the Judge asked.

"Hell, no," Fargo snapped.

The Judge made a face as though he were sucking a lemon and turned to one of the Sheriff's deputies. "Bring Miss Alma Ellison in," he said.

The deputy disappeared into an ante-room and

came back with a young woman, light-brown hair hanging to her shoulders. Fargo saw full, red lips, a snub nose, round cheeks and light-brown eyes that flicked a glance at him. She was pretty in a pouty sort of way, an air to the way she moved, a kind of unstated challenge. She wore a checked red and white dress with frills at the shoulders that made her seem younger than she was. It touched lightly on modest breasts, fell against slightly broad hips. "State your name," Judge Harrigan said.

"Alma Ellison," the young woman said.

The Judge held up a Bible. "You swear to tell the truth and nothin' but the truth?" he intoned and Alma Ellison nodded, said "yes" in a barely audible voice.

"Now you tell me what you saw happen last night with your own eyes," the Judge said.

Fargo watched Alma Ellison and caught the quick glance she threw at him and he frowned inwardly. The light-brown eyes held something veiled inside them, tiny pinpoints of fire that didn't match the outward calm she showed. "I was asleep," Alma began. "When voices near my window woke me up. I got up to see and there was our foreman, Max Twohey, arguing with a man. They were between my window and the barn. Then the other man suddenly pulled out a gun and shot Max twice, in cold blood. It was awful." Fargo watched as Alma Ellison paused to regain her composure and once again her eyes flicked to him.

"What happened then, Alma?" the Judge asked soothingly.

"The other man bent over Max. 'Nobody argues with Fargo,' he said," alma told the Judge.

"That's a goddamn lie," Fargo shouted.

The Judge's puckered face turned severe. "You be quiet. You'll have your turn," he said and banged the gavel on the bench. He returned his watery-blue eyes to Alma. "Go on, my dear, finish. What else did you see?" he questioned.

Fargo saw Alma swallow, lift her chin high. "The man who killed Max rode away on an Ovaro," she said. Fargo heard the curse escape his lips and as Alma turned away from the bench, her eyes met his for a brief instant. The tiny pinpoints were still there, he saw, and her prettiness had grown more pouty. She sat down in a chair near her father. He brought his attention back to the Judge as he heard the man's words directed at him.

"Now what've you got to say, Fargo?" the Judge questioned.

"It's a damn lie, all of it," Fargo said.

"You do ride an Ovaro," the Judge said.

"Sure but it's not the only Ovaro in the west," Fargo protested.

"Maybe not but they sure ain't common as chickweed, are they?" the Judge retorted. "I'd say two men right here near Bull Moose on the same night both riding an Ovaro would be a hell of a long coincidence."

"You going to convict a man on coincidence?" Fargo frowned.

"We've an eyewitness who heard you say your name," the Judge said.

"She heard wrong or she's a damn liar," Fargo roared.

The Judge turned and beckoned to Alma Ellison and the girl came forward. "Alma, you see the man you saw last night in this here courtroom now?" he asked.

Fargo watched with angry disbelief as Alma Ellison turned her pouty face to him, saw her lift her arm and point her finger. "Yes, Your Honor, that's him right there," she said.

"You little bitch," Fargo flung at her, started toward her and found the two deputies with their six-guns pressed into his ribs. They pushed him back and he moved with them but his eyes bored into Alma Ellison. She blinked, looked away from him.

"I'd say this does it," the Judge said. "Bring the prisoner forward." Fargo felt the two deputies take his arms as they pushed him in front of the bench and he saw Sheriff Mayberry come to stand behind him. "You've been identified as the man who killed Max Twohey by an eyewitness, a respectable young woman," the Judge said. "And other evidence of the kind called circumstantial backs her story to the hilt."

"I didn't do it. This is a goddamn frame-up," Fargo interrupted angrily.

The Judge's puckered countenance took on a chiding expression. "Can you give me any reason why this young woman would want to frame you for murder?" he asked.

Fargo felt his lips press hard against each other as the logic of the question dug deep. "No," he muttered. "Unless she's just plumb crazy and gets her kicks this way." He saw Sam Ellison jump to his feet, his square face flushed.

"You don't talk about my Alma that way, you murderin' bastard," the man shouted as others held him back. Fargo's eyes went to the girl. She sat quiet as a churchmouse, hands in her lap, eyes down and Fargo wondered if maybe he hadn't hit on something. The Judge's voice brought his attention back as Sam Ellison sat down.

"Having considered all the evidence in this case, I find you, Skye Fargo, guilty of murdering Max Twohey," the Judge intoned. "We don't tolerate that kind of thing here. Come dawn tomorrow, you shall be hanged by the neck until you are dead. Case closed." The Judge banged the gavel once and rose to his feet and Fargo felt the Sheriff's rifle in his back. His glance went to Alma Ellison as she rose, started to leave the room with her father. Her eyes flicked to him, the briefest of glances, and he saw a flash of something, almost apologetic, in the exchange. He watched her leave as he was taken from the room. Not a crazy, he muttered to himself. Not in the usual sense. But something, he grunted. It was in her eyes.

Excerpt from RED RIVER REVENGE

"Same cell," Sheriff Mayberry said and Fargo walked into the cell and heard the door slam shut behind him. He drew a deep sigh of frustration and anger. He was in jail, sentenced to be hung for a killing he didn't commit, fingered by a pouty young woman he'd never seen before. None of it made any damn sense.

Fargo opened his eyes and lifted himself onto one elbow on the narrow cot, shut off thoughts. He'd relived it a half-dozen times since morning and hadn't been able to find a thing to explain any of it. This last time had been no better than the others. Alma Ellison remained the key and one question above all others kept prodding at him. Why him? Why'd she pick him for her lies? And again, he could find no answer. He let his thoughts reach to Bowdon where the job waited and he couldn't see how that fitted in anywhere. Damn, he swore as he swung to his feet and went to the bars, peered out the window into the dark night. Sheriff Mayberry had relieved his young blond deputy and sat behind his desk with his feet up. Fargo saw the man eye him and stroke his gray mustache thoughtfully.

"Heard your name, Fargo. Heard you're the best Trailsman in the whole damn west. Why'd you come here and shoot Max? Have a grudge against him from way back sometime?"

"I hate people with the name Max, shoot 'em whenever I can," Fargo answered.

"You're one for smart answers, aren't you?" the Sheriff said. "Maybe if you'd told Judge Harrigan the truth he'd have gone easier on you."

"I told him the goddamn truth," Fargo spit out. His eyes roamed across the small ante-room, lingered on the case where his Colt and rifle were locked. He still had the throwing knife concealed in the leather sheath strapped around his calf. But it'd do him no good now. The Sheriff was too far away. Fargo's eyes went to the door of the jailhouse, peered out the window in it to the darkness outside. His one chance remained with the dawn, when they'd take him to the gallows. He'd have to make a break for it then and he heard the bitterness in the oath that curled inside him. It'd be a damn small chance. They'd be watching him like hawks around a chicken yard. His thoughts snapped off as the front door opened and he saw the girl enter, felt his mouth drop open. Alma Ellison carried a rattan basket with a cover on it and Sheriff Mayberry rose to his feet at once.

"Alma," the Sheriff questioned.

"I've brought him a last meal," Alma said, gesturing with her head toward the cell. "Daddy and I thought it the Christian thing to do."

"Well, that's mighty fine of you, Alma," the Sheriff said.

"May I just give it to him, Sheriff?" Alma said and Fargo saw her light-brown eyes focus on him, the tiny pinpoints inside them now little unmistakable fires. Her pretty poutiness remained and her full, red lips glistened. She peered hard at him and he frowned back, unable to read the strange lights in her eyes. She came toward him with the covered basket and Fargo saw the Sheriff take his six-gun out, hold it on him as he opened the cell door just enough for her to slide the basket inside. "Please eat this," Alma said to Fargo as she put the basket down on the floor. "I fixed it myself for you. Please."

She stepped back as the Sheriff slammed the door shut and Fargo stepped to the basket, picked it up. He opened the cover, saw the dish of fried chicken and the towel half-over it and beside it, the Walker Colt. He stared down at the gun, kept the astonishment from his face with an effort, lifted his eyes to Alma Ellison. She returned his stare, her eyes steady, the little lights burning in their light-brown orbs. Fargo stared down at the gun again. *Goddamn*, he breathed silently. *Goddamn!*

JOIN THE *TRAILSMAN* READERS' PANEL

Help us bring you more of the books you like by filling out this survey and mailing it in today.

1. Book title:_____

Book #:_____

2. Using the scale below how would you rate this book on the following features.

Poor		Not so Good			O.K.			Good		Excellent
0	1	2	3	4	5	6	7	8	9	10

Rating

Overall opinion of book..........................._____
Plot/Story ...._____
Setting/Location ...._____
Writing Style ...._____
Character Development ...._____
Conclusion/Ending ...._____
Scene on Front Cover ...._____

3. On average about how many western books do you buy for yourself each month?_____

4. How would you classify yourself as a reader of westerns?
I am a ( ) light ( ) medium ( ) heavy reader.

5. What is your education?
( ) High School (or less)   ( ) 4 yrs. college
( ) 2 yrs. college   ( ) Post Graduate

6. Age_____   **7.** Sex: ( ) Male ( ) Female

Please Print Name_____

Address_____

City_____State_____Zip_____

Phone # (   )_____

Thank you. Please send to New American Library, Research Dept, 1633 Broadway, New York, NY 10019.

Exciting Westerns by Jon Sharpe from SIGNET

*Price is $2.95 in Canada

**Buy them at your local
bookstore or use coupon
on next page for ordering.**

SIGNET Westerns You'll Enjoy

(0451)

☐ **CIMARRON #1: CIMARRON AND THE HANGING JUDGE** by Leo P. Kelley.
(120582—$2.50)*

☐ **CIMARRON #2: CIMARRON RIDES THE OUTLAW TRAIL** by Leo P. Kelley.
(120590—$2.50)*

☐ **CIMARRON #3: CIMARRON AND THE BORDER BANDITS** by Leo P. Kelley.
(122518—$2.50)*

☐ **CIMARRON #4: CIMARRON IN THE CHEROKEE STRIP** by Leo P. Kelley.
(123441—$2.50)*

☐ **CIMARRON #5: CIMARRON AND THE ELK SOLDIERS** by Leo P. Kelley.
(124898—$2.50)*

☐ **CIMARRON #6: CIMARRON AND THE BOUNTY HUNTERS** by Leo P. Kelley.
(125703—$2.50)*

☐ **CIMARRON #7: CIMARRON AND THE HIGH RIDER** by Leo P. Kelley.
(126866—$2.50)*

☐ **CIMARRON #8: CIMARRON IN NO MAN'S LAND** by Leo P. Kelley.
(128230—$2.50)*

☐ **CIMARRON #9: CIMARRON AND THE VIGILANTES** by Leo P. Kelley.
(129180—$2.50)*

☐ **CIMARRON #10: CIMARRON AND THE MEDICINE WOLVES** by Leo P. Kelley.
(130618—$2.50)*

☐ **LUKE SUTTON: OUTLAW** by Leo P. Kelley. (115228—$1.95)*

☐ **LUKE SUTTON: GUNFIGHTER** by Leo P. Kelley. (122836—$2.25)*

☐ **LUKE SUTTON: INDIAN FIGHTER** by Leo P. Kelley. (124553—$2.25)*

☑ **LUKE SUTTON: AVENGER** by Leo P. Kelley. (128796—$2.25)*

☐ **THE HALF-BREED** by Mick Clumpner. (112814—$1.95)*

☐ **MASSACRE AT THE GORGE** by Mick Clumpner. (117433—$1.95)*

*Prices slightly higher in Canada
